"I CAN'T BELIEVE WE ONLY MET AGAIN TWO WEEKS AGO."

Michael's lips were smiling, but his dark eyes remained grave.

Patsy took a deep breath. "Michael, there's something I have to tell you. I love you. I don't want to burden you or make you feel guilty, but I do love you, and that's never going to change."

When he finally spoke, his voice was strained, and a muscle flickered in his cheek. "Do you know that I have dreamed all my life of hearing you say those words?"

Suddenly Michael was looking at her as if she were a miracle. . . .

D1453338

JOAN WOLF is a native of New York City who currently resides in Connecticut with her husband and two children. She taught high school English in New York for nine years and took up writing when she retired to raise a family. She is the author of five other Rapture Romances, *Summer Storm, Change of Heart, Beloved Stranger, Affair of the Heart,* and *Portrait of a Love.*

Dear Reader:

We at Rapture Romance hope you will continue to enjoy our four books each month as much as we enjoy bringing them to you. Our commitment remains strong to giving you only the best, by well-known favorite authors and exciting new writers.

We've used the comments and opinions we've heard from *you*, the reader, to make our selections, so please keep writing to us. Your letters have already helped us bring you better books—the kind you want—and we appreciate and depend on them. Of course, we are always happy to forward mail to our authors—writers need to hear from their fans!

Happy reading!

The Editors
Rapture Romance
New American Library
1633 Broadway
New York, NY 10019

A FASHIONABLE AFFAIR

by
Joan Wolf

RAPTURE ROMANCE
NEW AMERICAN LIBRARY

PUBLISHER'S NOTE

This novel is a work of fiction. Names, characters, places, and incidents either are the product of the author's imagination or are used fictitiously, and any resemblance to actual persons, living or dead, events, or locales is entirely coincidental.

NAL BOOKS ARE AVAILABLE AT QUANTITY DISCOUNTS
WHEN USED TO PROMOTE PRODUCTS OR SERVICES.
FOR INFORMATION PLEASE WRITE TO PREMIUM MARKETING DIVISION,
NEW AMERICAN LIBRARY, 1633 BROADWAY,
NEW YORK, NEW YORK 10019.

SIGNET, SIGNET CLASSIC, MENTOR, PLUME, MERIDIAN and NAL BOOKS
are published by New American Library,
1633 Broadway, New York, New York 10019

First Printing, February, 1985

1 2 3 4 5 6 7 8 9

PRINTED IN THE UNITED STATES OF AMERICA

Chapter One

Patsy Clark flashed a bright, friendly smile at the doorman, entered the elevator, and rode up to her sixth-floor apartment. She was frowning slightly, however, as she let herself in, and as she closed the door behind her the telephone rang. Patsy went into the kitchen and picked up the extension.

"Hello," she said in her clear, low-pitched voice.

"May I speak to Miss Patricia Clark, please. This is the Internal Revenue Service calling."

Patsy's eyes widened. "This is she," she said, and abruptly sat down.

"Miss Clark, this is John Maginnis. We've been looking into your tax return and there are a few things I'd like to go over with you. May I come and see you some time this week?"

There was a blank pause. "Well, of course," Patsy said, breaking the silence. "But I'm afraid I don't know very much about my taxes, Mr. Maginnis. My business manager, Fred Zimmerman, handles all that."

"Your business manager can be present when I talk to you."

"But that's just the problem," Patsy explained. "He can't. He's in the hospital. In fact, I've just come from visiting him. He's had a heart attack."

"I see." The cool voice on the other end of the line was very pleasant but distinctly businesslike. "Well, perhaps you'll be able to answer my questions yourself, Miss Clark. Could you see me tomorrow?"

"Not tomorrow. I have a modelling session. Wednesday would be all right."

"Wednesday, then. At ten o'clock?"

"All right. Should I come to your office?"

"No." He sounded quite definite. "I'll come to your apartment. Thank you, Miss Clark."

"Good-bye," Patsy said faintly. She stood up to replace the receiver and remained staring at the old-fashioned wall phone for a few moments. "Damn!" she said. She went into the living room and threw herself on the sofa.

Should she tell Fred? She thought of his sickly gray face on the pillow this afternoon and decided almost immediately not to. She would just have to deal with this IRS man herself. After all, she thought righteously, whatever could they find wrong? She paid an absolutely *huge* amount of taxes each year. The audit was probably only routine. Then, being Patsy, she banished the whole thing from her mind and went inside to change for a dinner date.

Her doorbell rang promptly at ten o'clock Wednesday morning and Patsy went to the door to let the IRS man in. "Mr. Maginnis?" she said.

"Yes." The man's eyes widened slightly in a familiar expression of shocked delight as he looked for the first time at Patricia Clark. He took in her red hair, so fine that it floated around her shoulders like a luminous cloud; her wide brown eyes, so unbelievably dark in the dazzling purity of her flawless face. He had, of course, seen her photographs, but the reality was still astonishing.

Patsy held the door wider. "Come in," she said. She was wearing tan slacks and a tattersall shirt with the sleeves rolled up. Being almost as tall as he, she smiled directly into his eyes. Patsy was well accustomed to the effect she had on men. "Would you like a cup of coffee?"

The IRS however, is made of stern stuff. John Maginnis' face resumed its impersonal look. "No, thank you," he said in a colorless voice. "Perhaps we could just get down to business."

Patsy sighed. "All right. Do you want to sit at a table?"

"That would be helpful."

"Come into the kitchen, then."

The agent's eyes darted appraisingly around the apartment as she led him down the hall and into a big, immaculate, fully equipped kitchen. Patsy sat at a white Formica table and gestured for him to do likewise. He opened his briefcase and took out a file folder. Then he began to ask her some questions.

Fifteen minutes later Patsy was staring at a sheet of figures in utter frustration.

"I'm afraid it's no good, Mr. Maginnis," she said, putting the paper down. "To be honest, I don't understand a word you're saying. If you say I own shares in this Fairmont Shopping Center, then I probably do. Fred is always buying me shares of shopping centers." She raised her eyes to the agent's unconcerned face. "He's always told me it's a perfectly legal tax shelter."

"It is, Miss Clark. But this particular shopping center has been oversold, you see, and so we are disallowing this deduction."

"Oh," Patsy said. "Do you mean I owe you more taxes?"

"I'm afraid so, Miss Clark."

"I see," Patsy replied thinking bitter thoughts about the taxes she had already paid.

"You said you owned shares in a number of shopping centers, Miss Clark?"

"Yes."

"I think, purely as a matter of routine, that I'd like to take a look into those investments."

Patsy stared at Maginnis. "But I've already told you, my business manager is in the hospital. You'll have to wait until he recovers."

The IRS man gathered his papers and placed them in his briefcase. "I'd like to finish with this as soon as possible, Miss Clark."

"But Fred is in the *hospital*," Patsy repeated. "I simply cannot bother him right now."

"Then I suggest you get yourself an accountant,

Miss Clark," the agent said pleasantly but firmly. "I'll call you next week."

"Next week," Patsy shrieked glaring at him in outrage.

A gleam of appreciation flickered in Maginnis' cool blue eyes, but he repeated evenly, "Next week. Get an accountant, Miss Clark. Thank you and good morning."

Patsy closed the door behind him and stalked back into the living room. "I don't believe this," she said out loud, and walked to the long window that overlooked Central Park. The trees and grass were green with spring. "I don't *know* any accountants," Patsy said. She put her hands into her pockets and remained at the window, watching a group of children bicycle across Central Park West and enter the park. A thoughtful look descended over her face.

"Michael," she said. "Michael is an accountant."

She left the living room and went down another hall and into her bedroom. Sitting behind a maple desk, Patsy picked up the phone and dialed a number. It was answered on the sixth ring.

"Sally," Patsy said. "Thank goodness you're in."

"I was in the basement doing laundry," her long-time best friend answered. "What's up, Patsy? You sound upset."

"I am, rather. I've just had an IRS man here and they want to audit me."

"Well, that's never pleasant, of course, but it's no reason to get yourself into a tizzy." Sally's voice changed. "No, Steven, you may not have that lollipop. It's much too early."

"You don't understand, Sal. Fred is in the hospital. He had a heart attack a few days ago."

"Fred? I didn't know that. How old is he, Patsy?"

"Only fifty."

"Oh, dear. Is it bad?"

"I'm afraid so. The doctors said if he hadn't gotten to the hospital when he did, he'd be dead."

"Good God."

"Yes. So, under the circumstances, I can hardly expect him to cope with the IRS. I tried to explain that elementary fact to the IRS man who was here, but all he said was 'Get an accountant.' "

"Lord."

"Sally, Michael's an accountant. I know he works for the government, but do you think he might help me? Or at least recommend someone who could?"

"Michael's not working for the Justice Department anymore," Sally said. "He's just gone into partnership with an accountant out here on the Island. I'm sure he could help you, Patsy. If there's anyone who has had experience in dealing with the IRS, it's my darling brother."

"I know," Patsy said. "But he's always been on the other end!"

Sally laughed. "True." There was the sound of banging in the background. "Steven, no!" Sally said. "You're frightening the baby."

"Do you have Michael's work number?" Patsy asked.

"Yes. Hold on a minute." There was the sound of the phone being put down and Patsy accurately pictured the scene in Sally's kitchen. Sally retrieved the phone. "Here it is." She dictated a number, and Patsy wrote it down.

"Thank's a million, Sally," she said. "I'll call him right away."

"Okay. Let me know how things work out."

"I will. And thanks again. Give the kids a hug and a kiss for me."

"You come out soon and hug and kiss for yourself."

"I will. 'Bye."

Patsy hung up and left the receiver on the hook for half a minute before lifting it again, this time putting in a call to the CPA partnership of Lawson and Melville in West Hampstead, Long Island.

At three o'clock that afternoon Patsy drove her Volvo station wagon over the Triborough Bridge out of Manhattan and onto Long Island. She negotiated the maze of highways with easy confidence— Patsy had, after all, grown up on Long Island—and cruised comfortably along the Long Island Expressway until she saw the sign for West Hampstead. She got off the expressway and followed the directions Michael had given her over the phone. In five minutes she was parking her car in a small lot behind an old, three-story clapboard house.

There wasn't a cloud on Patsy's lovely face as she smiled at the receptionist and asked for Michael. When she was told he'd be with her in a minute, she nodded serenely and sat on the sofa in the waiting area. She picked up a magazine, which happened to have her picture on the cover, and thumbed through it, utterly unaware of the receptionist's envious eyes.

Twenty minutes went by. Patsy put down the magazine and looked around.

"I'm sorry it's taking so long, Miss Clark," the receptionist said apologetically, "but Mr. Melville is with another client."

Patsy smiled. "I don't mind waiting. It was good of him to squeeze me in at such short notice." She stood and the folds of her emerald green suit skirt fell gracefully around her long legs. "I hope you don't mind if I prowl about for a bit."

"Of course not," the girl answered.

There was the sound of male voices in the hall and then a tall, broad-shouldered man entered the reception room. He was in his early thirties, very good-looking, and his blue eyes instantly glued themselves to Patsy. Miss Revere, the receptionist, had been trying vainly for weeks to cadge a date with him, and her lips tightened in frustration as she observed the bedazzled expression in his eyes.

Patsy, however, had barely noticed him. Her eyes were on the shorter, slender, dark-haired man who now stood in the doorway.

"Well, Patsy," said a deep, slightly amused voice. "I'd know that red hair anywhere."

Patsy laughed and crossed the room with the swift, graceful walk so familiar to fans of her TV commercials.

"Michael!" she said, holding out her hands. "I do appreciate you seeing me like this, really I do."

"It's a pleasure," he said easily, briefly clasping her hands. "Come into my office and tell me all about it."

Patsy obediently followed him down a hall, up a flight of stairs, and into a comfortable, unostentatious office. He gestured for her to sit in the chair in front of his desk, and he himself sat behind it. Leaning back a bit, he regarded her out of darkly lashed hazel eyes. "It's been a long time, " he said.

Patsy was conscious of a shock of deep surprise. The man facing her seemed very different from the Michael she remembered. She frowned a little. "Yes, it has been," she said slowly. "I'm trying to remember when I last saw you."

"It was at my father's funeral."

Her eyes widened. "Was it as long ago as that?"

"Seven years." His voice was cool and steady, his eyes level and inscrutable.

"Seven years," Patsy repeated. "My God." She wrinkled her nose. "Do you know that in two years I'll be thirty? Can you believe it? Do you remember how *old* we used to think thirty was?"

He grinned and suddenly looked much younger, much more like the Michael she remembered. "It seems younger every day," he said.

"Well, you at least have three more years before the bell tolls," she retorted.

"You're depressing the hell out of me, Patsy," he complained humorously, and Patsy laughed.

"Sorry," she apologized, "but I've been smitten by melancholy all day. The IRS can do that to you."

The humor left Michael's face, and he leaned back slightly in his chair. "Tell me about it."

After a brief hesitation Patsy recounted the entire story and then answered the few questions he asked her as clearly and intelligently as she could. The phone rang. "Excuse me," Michael said, picking up the receiver. As he spoke, his attention on the conversation, Patsy looked searchingly at his face and tried to figure out why he seemed so different when so much about him was familiar. The black hair was the same as were the hazel eyes, the high-bridged nose and straight, firm mouth. But it was not a boy's face any longer. Nor was the voice—cool, pleasant, subtly authoritative—the same as the voice she remembered, even though so many of the intonations were familiar.

He hung up, and his eyes returned to her. "The first thing I'll have to do," he said, "is look at your past tax returns."

"Fred Zimmerman has all those records, Michael."

"Where's his office?"

"On East Forty-fourth Street."

"Can you get the key from him?"

"I guess so. He's still in the hospital, poor guy."

"Too bad." Michael's darkly lashed greenish eyes were quite impersonal. "Patsy, do you know how much money you made last year?"

Patsy lowered her eyes. "Something over two million dollars," she answered softly.

Michael did not blink. "I see. And Fred was investing it for you?"

"Yes." Patsy felt like a school girl being brought

before the principal, and to shake her unease she smiled at Michael. "He put a lot of money into shopping-center shares," she said. "Unfortunately, it seems one of them was not quite on the up and up."

"I see." He did not return her smile. In fact, he looked rather preoccupied. His face was thinner than she remembered, Patsy thought. Or perhaps it was just that his shoulders were wider. "Well, there isn't much I can do until I get a look at those records," he said, and Patsy's eyes guiltily snapped back to his face. "Why don't you go see this Zimmerman fellow and give me a call tomorrow if you have the key to his office. I'll meet you there and we'll see what we can come up with."

"All right," Patsy said, and then, belatedly, realized she was being dismissed. She stood up. "Thank you, Michael."

He had risen with her. "Not at all." The phone rang again. "Can you find your way out?" he asked.

"Of course."

He was picking up the receiver as she left.

Chapter Two

~

Patsy hit rush-hour traffic on the way home, so she had plenty of time to think about her interview with Michael Melville. She didn't waste any thoughts on her tax problems; what she thought about was Michael—the boy she had grown up with, Sally's little brother.

The Clark and the Melville families had lived next door to each other on Long Island since their children had been born. Sally was the oldest, then Patsy, and then Michael. As only eighteen months separated Sally and Michael, the children were virtually the same age and had played together since the time they could talk. It wasn't until they had gotten into junior high that Patsy had started to think of Michael as being younger than she. Because of the way their birthdays fell, Patsy was in Sally's class—a year ahead of Michael. And that year assumed gigantic proportions as they grew older.

But they had always been good friends. It was Michael, brilliant in math and in an accelerated program, who had drummed the rudiments of trig-onometry into Patsy's head. Sally, also a top math student, had not had the patience. And when Michael had been state wrestling champion in his junior year, Patsy had been in the audience cheering him on.

Yet they had always been *just* friends. Patsy had dated constantly all through high school, but never with Michael.

Seven years, Patsy thought. Had it really been seven years since she had seen him last?

She finally edged her car into the toll booth on the Triborough, handed the man her money, and accelerated slowly. If Sally hadn't married a med-ical student and moved to Michigan, Patsy thought, she and Michael would have met more often. Now that Sally was back home, no doubt they would be seeing a bit more of each other. Seven years, thought Patsy. My goodness. Where had the time gone to?

That evening after dinner Patsy went to the hos-pital to see her business manager. He had been moved from the intensive-care unit into a regular private room and she sat with him for a few minutes chatting about insignificant things before asking him for the key to his office.

He frowned. "What do you need that for?"

"Oh," she deliberately kept her tone light and unconcerned. "There are a few papers I need. There's nothing to worry about, Fred."

"The hospital took all my keys when I was admitted," he said slowly. "I don't know where they've put them."

Patsy got to her feet. "I'll find out."

She was gone for ten minutes, and when she came back, she was with a woman who was holding his keys.

"Here they are, Fred," Patsy said serenely. "Just show me the office key, and we'll send the rest back."

He separated out a key and very slowly gave the chain to Patsy. She detached the key he had indicated and gave the rest to the woman, who smiled coolly and departed. Patsy sat next to his bed.

"I have my first shooting on the new camera contract on Monday," she said. "It should be fun."

"Yeah." Fred was clearly not paying attention. "Patsy, what's up? Why do you want that key?"

He looked really disturbed and Patsy decided that he would probably worry more if he didn't know what was going on.

"It's nothing major. Fred, I promise you. I had an IRS man come by the other day. He was asking questions about my investment in the Fairmont Shopping Center."

Fred seemed to relax. "Oh, Fairmont. So, what's wrong with it?"

"He said it was oversold, whatever that means, and they are not allowing my deduction."

"Oversold," Fred repeated. "Well, I'll be damned."

"Yes. He wanted to see my old tax returns as well. That's why I need the key."

"You mean this IRS guy wants to talk to you again?"

"Yes. But it's purely routine, Fred. He said so."

Fred tried to sit up straight in bed. "Patsy, listen. I'll give you the name of a guy to get in touch with. He'll help you go through the files and get the material."

Patsy gently pressed him down onto his back. "Don't worry about a thing, Fred. I've already got someone—an old friend from Long Island who happens to be a CPA. He's going to get the tax material together."

Fred let her push him against the pillow. "Oh. A fellow from Long Island. What's his name?"

"Michael Melville."

Fred frowned. "Michael Melville. I know that name."

"He used to work for the Justice Department here in New York," Patsy said helpfully. "He's in private practice in Long Island now."

Patsy had thought Fred looked gray when she came in but now his skin turned the shade of parchment. "Jesus," he said. "*That* Melville."

"Are you all right, Fred?" Patsy asked anxiously.

He put his hand to his chest. "I'm fine," he said. "Patsy, listen to me . . ." But Patsy had gone for the nurse.

Later that night Fred Zimmerman suffered another massive heart attack and died.

It was a very subdued Patsy who called Michael the following morning.

"I'm sorry to hear that," he said neutrally when she told him of Fred's death.

"The thing is, Michael, I feel as if I've killed him," she confessed. "I should never have told him about the IRS."

"Patsy, be reasonable. He'd already had one massive attack. The other had probably been building all day."

"Do you think so?"

"Of course. Accountants deal with the IRS all the time. He wasn't upset about the IRS. He was having a heart attack."

Patsy's brow smoothed out. She was never one to dwell on unpleasant or upsetting thoughts. "You're probably right."

"Sure I am. Now, can you meet me at his office this afternoon?"

"Yes. Fred has a daughter, and she's taking care of the arrangements. What time can you be there?"

"Three o'clock. What's the address again?"

She gave it to him, hung up the phone, and went to jog in Central Park.

He was waiting in the lobby when she arrived. He was wearing a well-cut, pale-gray suit, and once again Patsy found herself gazing appraisingly at his shoulders. Michael had always been slender and compact, but even in high school he had been strong. She remembered he had once beaten up the captain of the football team for saying something disparaging about a thin, bespeckled, academically minded friend of his.

His dark head turned and he saw her.

"Have you been waiting long?" she asked as she approached him.

"No, I just got here." He put a hand on her elbow. "The elevator is over here."

Obediently she fell into step beside him. She was wearing medium-high heels with her chocolate-colored slacks and cream sweater, and he was still nearly an inch taller than she. "Did you drive in?" she asked.

"No. I took the train."

"That was probably smart. It doesn't pay to bring a car into Manhattan. I only have one because I can garage it in my apartment building."

"Was that your Volvo wagon I saw in the parking lot yesterday?"

"Yes."

The elevator door opened and they started down the corridor. "A station wagon," he said with amusement in his deep, pleasant voice. "Not at all the sort of car one would expect to see New York's top photographic model driving."

"It's built like a tank," Patsy said. "New York's top photographic model is more interested in protection than in style, thank you."

"Smart girl," he said. "Here we are." He fitted the key into the lock and they entered Fred's office.

An hour later Michael was sitting at Fred's desk with a pile of folders in front of him. Patsy, who was finding the whole process extremely boring, was prowling around the office.

"Sit down, Red," Michael said absently. "You're making me nervous."

Red. She had forgotten that. He was the only one she had ever allowed to call her by that name. She crossed the room and sat across the desk from him, her eyes on his preoccupied face. He had always had the most fabulous lashes, she remembered. She and Sally had been wild with jealousy when they were younger. "I mean, what good are they on a boy?" Sally used to say.

"*Patsy*. Are you awake?" There was a distinct note of irritation in Michael's voice, and she opened her brown eyes wide.

"I'm sorry, I was daydreaming. What did you say?"

"I asked you about this line of sportswear you're endorsing. I've never heard of the company."

"Redman Fashions," she answered readily. "I know they're not Sears, but the clothes have really been very successful."

"I see that." There was a thin deep line between his eyes. He was looking at the paper in front of him. "You made over a million from them last year."

She smiled. "You see."

He looked from the paper to her. "I've never seen them in the stores," he said.

"Neither have I, actually. But Fred said they were very popular in the smaller Midwest department stores."

"I see." Michael's voice was undramatic and his

face unreadable. "Have you ever seen any of these shopping centers Fred invested in?"

"No, of course not. They're all somewhere in the Midwest."

Michael's brows rose and he looked at her in momentary silence.

Patsy gave him a charming, rueful look. "Oh, dear, I don't mean to sound like an ugly New Yorker."

"No one will ever call you an ugly anything, sweetheart," he said, returning his attention to her papers.

Patsy found herself thrown a bit off balance. She frowned and studied his absorbed face, trying to figure out what was so different about him.

He was older, of course, but that wasn't it. There was an authoritative air about him that the boy had not had, a quality of quiet power. She looked at the thin dark face.

The long lashes lifted. "Everything seems to be in order, but I'm going to have to do some checking," he said. "Is it all right if I take your files back to my own office?"

"Of course it's all right." She looked at the files heaped on the desk. "You're never going to get all that home on the train."

"I'm planning," he explained calmly, "to borrow your car."

"Oh, are you?"

"Yes." He stood up. "Come on, we'll go back to your apartment and collect it. I'll drive it back in for you tomorrow morning."

Patsy followed him to the door. It occurred to her that she had been hopping to his orders since yesterday afternoon. "Fortunately, I don't need the car tonight," she said a trifle acidly.

"Fortunately," he agreed with perfect composure, and held the door open for her.

They took a taxi to Patsy's apartment. It was rush hour and the streets were clogged with traffic.

"You don't want to drive in this madhouse," Patsy said as they got out of the cab. "Why don't you let me fix you some dinner and you can leave when things have calmed down."

"Great," he said instantly.

Patsy laughed. "Don't let me twist your arm."

He grinned. "Six months out of New York and I'm reverting to being a hick. This traffic gives me the willies."

Patsy felt a stab of irritation. She was not accustomed to men regarding her as a mere refuge from rush-hour traffic.

"You're sure I'm not keeping you from another engagement?" he asked as they walked toward her front door.

As a matter of fact, Patsy was planning to cancel her date as soon as she could get to the phone. "Nothing important," she said airily. "Lucky for you I've got a steak in the freezer."

"Lucky for me," he repeated amiably, following her into the lobby.

She left Michael fixing drinks in the kitchen and went into her bedroom to make her call.

"Hi, Don," she said to the man on the other end

of the wire. "I'm afraid I'm going to have to break our date tonight." She listened for a few minutes, her eyes fixed on a favorite landscape hanging on the pale golden bedroom wall. "I know," she said at last. "And I'm terribly, terribly sorry. But the IRS is going to audit me, and I have to huddle with my accountant. It's all too dreadful, Don. Fred died last night. He had another heart attack." She listened again, her foot tapping lightly on the thick beige carpet. "Yes," she said, "I know. I'll call you when things straighten out a bit. Yes. I know you do, Don. All right. Good-bye." Patsy hung up briskly and went into the kitchen.

Michael had taken off his suit jacket and hung it over the back of a kitchen chair. In his shirt sleeves he looked much stronger than one would have supposed. Patsy, however, was not surprised. "Why don't you take off your tie too?" she said. She picked up her drink and took a sip while he did as she suggested. "Do you remember the time you beat up Dean Walters?" she asked unexpectedly.

He unbuttoned the top button of his shirt and looked at her in surprise. "Dean Walters?" he repeated. "Your old boyfriend?"

"The same."

"Yeah. Whatever brought that to your mind?"

"Seeing you in your shirt sleeves," Patsy replied with disconcerting candor.

He looked startled at first, and then began to smile. "Dean Walters was a swine," he said, taking a long sip of his drink.

"He was," Patsy agreed cordially. "And he wasn't my boyfriend for very long."

"True." He looked at her out of inscrutable hazel eyes. "You never could bear anyone who wasn't kind."

"It doesn't take a great deal of effort to be pleasant," Patsy said lightly. She took the steak out of the freezer and put it on a countertop. Michael was looking around the kitchen.

"Do you have a view of the park from here?" he asked.

"Yes. From both the living room and the bedroom. Come on, I'll show you the rest of the apartment."

The drapes in the living room were open and the big, high-ceilinged room was filled with natural light. It was a comfortable room, with bookcases, plants, and chinz-covered furniture. Michael walked around the room, his thoughtful gaze taking in the good but certainly not fabulously expensive furniture. Just as Patsy was starting to get her back up, he turned to her and smiled. "It's a great room," he said. "I like it very much."

Immediately disarmed, she smiled back. "The rest of the apartment will probably look very familiar. When Mother and Daddy moved to Arizona, I inherited all the furniture they didn't want. Here's the dining room." And the dining room was indeed furnished with the Hitchcock set Michael remembered from her parents' home. "I've got my old maple bedroom set, too," Patsy informed him.

"And the twin beds from the spare room. Mother didn't want another big house, she said."

They were in the living room again and she gestured for him to sit down. He chose a club chair and Patsy subsided on the sofa, kicking off her shoes and pulling her legs up under her. Her red hair floated around her shoulders, glinting with copper and gold highlights. Her body was relaxed and unstudiedly graceful against the cushions, her flawless face clear in the afternoon light. She sipped her drink and gazed at him.

She had never had any vanity, he thought suddenly. She was so beautiful that she didn't need it.

"How are your parents?" he asked, revolving his glass in his hands.

"Pretty good. The move to Arizona was a good idea. Mother's arthritis is definitely better."

"Do you miss them?"

Patsy made a face. "I do. Isn't it silly? I haven't lived at home for years and during the week I never think about them, but come Sunday afternoon and it hits me that there's no mother to make me leg of lamb and mashed potatoes. I visit when I can, of course, but it isn't the same."

"No," he agreed. "That's one of the reasons Sally and Steve came back East, I think. Steve's parents aren't getting any younger, and Sally's only family is me." He smiled faintly. "And you," he added.

Patsy met his eyes and felt an odd little flutter in her stomach. "I'm glad she's back," she replied. "I missed her. I have other friends, of course, but there's no one like Sally." She laughed and tried to recover her balance. "When I think of my phone bills!"

He didn't say anything but continued to regard her, that faint smile still on his face. In order to cover her confusion, Patsy stood up. "Well, if we're going to eat, I'd better get to work."

He stood up as well. "I'll make a salad if you want."

"Great," Patsy said.

They prepared and ate the meal together in comfortable conversation, and by the time Patsy got up to make coffee, she felt as if she had the old Michael back.

"Did I tell you that Fred knew who you were?" she asked, stirring milk into her coffee.

He looked at her, his hazel eyes intent and narrow. "No," she said. "You didn't tell me."

"When I told him you used to be with the Justice Department. He said, 'Oh, *that* Melville.' "

"I see," Michael murmured.

"He must have heard about you catching that organized-crime bigshot on tax evasion."

"He must have," he agreed. His eyes were half-veiled by his lashes. "I'm surprised *you* knew about it," he said.

"Oh, I followed the whole thing in the papers. Sally told me you were the one who caught him."

"Yes. But my name never appeared in the papers."

"I know. But I knew, from Sally, who they were referring to when they spoke of the 'young Justice Department accountant,' you see."

"I see how *you* knew," he pointed out. "What I don't see is how Fred knew."

"Oh," Patsy said blankly. "Well, maybe he knew you from something else."

"Maybe," he replied blandly as he rose from the chair. "Everything was delicious, Patsy, but I'd better get going. I have to collect the stuff at the office first. Do you have the car keys?"

Patsy obediently went to fetch the keys and then took him to the garage. "Will you be home tomorrow morning for me to return it?" he asked.

"Yes, of course."

"Fine, I'll see you then." He opened the car door and got in. Patsy stepped back and watched as Michael competently backed the Volvo out of its space and proceeded up the ramp and out of the garage.

"Yes, sir," she said out loud, half in amusement and half in annoyance. Then she turned and went back upstairs.

Chapter Three

❧

Patsy got up early Saturday morning and went for a run in the park. She was just getting out of the shower when the phone rang. Wrapping a towel around herself, she went into the bedroom to answer it.

"Patsy?" said the voice on the other end.

She recognized it instantly. "Hi, Michael, What's up?"

"I'm afraid I have a rather hysterical client on my hands this morning. I'm not going to be able to get your car back to you after all."

He sounded quite matter-of-fact, not apologetic at all. "Oh," Patsy said. "Well, when do you think you'll be able to get in?"

"Not this afternoon, either. But I was talking to Sally earlier and she wondered if you'd come out to dinner. She'll meet you at the train. Then I'll drive the car to Sally's and you'll have it to get back home."

Patsy stared at the phone in disbelief. But her voice, when she spoke, was quite calm. "You want

me to take the train out to Sally's so I can collect my
own car, which you borrowed, because you don't
have the time to return it yourself."

"That's right." He sounded quite cheerful. "If
you can't make it, I'm afraid you'll have to wait for
the car."

"I'll come."

"Great. Sally said she'd give you a call this morning. See you later, then."

"See you later," Patsy repeated and hung up in a
slight state of shock. She had had no intention of
going to Long Island. Why did I say I'd come? she
asked herself. I don't need the car this weekend. I
should have made him bring it back tomorrow. She
shook her head in bewilderment at her own behavior and went over to her closet. I suppose it does
behoove me to be a little accommodating, she told
herself as she chose slacks and a blouse. After all, it
is very nice of Michael to take on my problem. And
it will be nice to see Sally and the kids.

She finished dressing and went back to the
phone. She was going to have to break another
date.

She took an afternoon train out of Penn Station.
Sally, as promised, was waiting for her at the Long
Island station.

"Hi, Sal," Patsy said, giving her best friend an
affectionate kiss.

Sally smiled, her hazel eyes bright with pleasure.
Strange, Patsy thought, she had never noticed that

Sally's eyes were the same color as Michael's. Michael's lashes, however, were definitely longer.

"I've got the gang," Sally said, gesturing to the two kids in the back carseats. She took Patsy's overnight bag and put it in the rear of the station wagon, then got into the driver's seat. Patsy slid in next to her and turned to grin at the children.

"Hi, Steven! How are you?"

"Hi, Aunt Patsy," the three-year-old returned with enthusiasm. "Did you bring me something?"

"Steven," his mother said despairingly.

Patsy laughed. "I did. And I brought something for my godchild, too. Hi, Matthew." The baby gurgled in reply.

"What is it?" Steven asked.

"You'll see when we get home," Patsy answered, and turned back to Sally. "Is Steve on duty today?" Steve Maxwell was an orthopedic surgeon at Long Island Medical Center on the north shore.

"Yes, but he should be home for dinner. Michael is coming too. He was sorry to put you to the trouble of coming out, but I'm glad you did. It's so good to see you."

Patsy hadn't thought he sounded at all sorry, but she refrained from saying so to Sally. "It's great to see you," she said instead, and meant it.

"Michael's very busy," his sister explained. "Last-minute tax returns, you know."

They chatted comfortably during the ten-minute ride to Sally's house, a big old colonial with a fenced-in yard containing a gas grill, picnic table, sandbox, and swing set.

"The house is looking great," Patsy commented as she looked around the front hall and the living room. "You had the floors done."

"Yes. Finally. And we had new linoleum put down in the kitchen. My next big job is to refinish all the doors."

Patsy was playing blocks with Steven on the floor of the family room when Michael came in. She didn't hear him at first. Sally was in the kitchen and had opened the door before he had even knocked. Michael stood for half a minute in the doorway watching her play with the little boy. She had a truck in her hand and was pushing it along a track they had built with the blocks. They were both making rumbling noises and Patsy was crawling on her hands and knees when she noticed a pair of Top-Siders in the doorway. She looked up and met a pair of amused hazel eyes. "Oh," she said. "I didn't know you were here."

"Well, I am," he replied amiably.

"Uncle Michael! Uncle Michael!" Steven shrieked, and hurled himself forward.

"Hi there, tiger," Michael said, swinging him up into his arms.

"Did you bring me anything?" Steven asked.

Patsy laughed and got to her feet. "He's got it down to a science."

"Of course I brought you something," Michael answered. He put his nephew down, reached into his pocket, and removed a small magnet and a penny.

Steven was absolutely delighted and raced off to show his mother.

"I brought him a long black cord from an old dress of mine," Patsy said. "He adored it. He was winding it around every doorknob in the house until we decided to play blocks."

Michael chuckled. "Between us, we're spoiling him to death."

Patsy dusted off the knees of her wide-wale corduroy pants and looked at him from under her lashes. They were very lovely lashes, artfully darkened and naturally long—almost as long as his. He really looked very fit in those chino slacks and navy Izod shirt, she thought.

"Did you manage to soothe your hysterical client?" she asked as she straightened up.

"Marginally. He got himself into a mess, I'm afraid."

"What did he do?"

"Tried to be clever with his taxes. It's going to cost him plenty to bail out."

"Oh, dear. I can understand why he was hysterical. Can you help him?"

"If he'll listen to me. The advice I'm giving him is good, but I rather doubt he's going to take it."

"He sounds like a nuisance," Patsy said frankly.

Michael shrugged. "My favorite clients are incompetent nuisances with their affairs in a mess."

"Like me?" Patsy asked sweetly.

"Like you. What's this racehorse I see you own?"

Patsy decided to go along with the change of subject. "Ebony Lad? He's a darling, and he's done

very well this year. He started to come on last fall.
Earl Hibbard, his trainer, says he's a late bloomer.
He was a bust at three, and now at four, he's
turning into a winner."

"And a tax deduction."

Patsy laughed. "Yes. And he's *much* more fun
than shopping-center shares."

"Uncle Michael!" Steven raced back into the
room, and in a few minutes he had both adults on
the floor playing blocks with him.

Sally fed the kids first and then put them to bed,
so when the four adults finally sat down to dinner,
peace reigned.

"I'm delighted to see you, Patsy," Steve said as
they ate Sally's delicious veal parmigiana, "but surprised. You don't usually spend your Saturday
nights so tamely."

"Yes," Sally added, "where's Don?"

"Sulking," Patsy replied.

"Did you stand him up?"

Patsy smiled and took a bite of her veal. "Terrific," she approved. "I told him I was having a
problem with my taxes." She shrugged gracefully.
"Really, he was quite petulant. Just like a little boy.
Or—no. Little Steven and Matthew aren't petulant
at all. They're much nicer than Don, in fact."

"Exit Don," Sally remarked dryly, and her husband laughed.

Patsy took another bite of veal. "Yes," she said, "I
rather think so." She looked at Sally's husband.
"How do you like the hospital, Steve?"

His blue eyes blazed. "It's great," he raved, and proceeded to tell her all about it.

Sally, seated across the table from her friend, turned to Michael. "I've got a particularly tricky math problem for you," she said. "One of the graduate assistants brought it to me and it's a beaut. Will you look at it after dinner?"

He looked suddenly alert. "Sure." He began to ask her questions and soon the two were involved in a highly technical, totally incomprehensible conversation.

"Do you still have that crazy cleaning woman?" Steve asked Patsy, abandoning the topic of the hospital.

"Who? Oh—May, do you mean? Yes. She still cleans my apartment, and yes, she's still trying to convert me."

"Convert you to what?" Michael asked, and Patsy, glad of an excuse to look at him, turned her head.

"She's an evangelical type, always trying to save me from my sinful life. Poor thing, she's a bit bonkers, I think."

"She's not only bonkers," Steve said, "she's damn offensive. I don't know how you put up with it."

"I usually try not to be home when she comes," Patsy replied. "The day you were in with the children was the last time I actually saw her."

"It's ridiculous," Steve said impatiently. "Why should you have to flee from your own house? Why don't you just hire someone else?"

"Because if I fire her, she'll be out of work. I mean, who else would put up with her, poor soul?

And the money she makes from me supplements her social-security check."

"Michael, do you remember Mr. Gerstner?" Sally asked.

"God, yes."

"Mr. Gerstner was another one of Patsy's sad cases," Sally explained to her husband. "He taught history at Central High, and he was a disaster. The kids literally ran wild in his room. Once some boys set a pigeon loose in the classroom—a real live pigeon."

Steve looked unimpressed. "So? Every school has an ineffective teacher like that."

"Patsy felt sorry for him," Sally continued. "She felt so sorry for him that she stood up in class during the third week we had him and told everybody off. It was quite impressive. Patsy, who never lost her temper at anything."

"Did they listen to you?" Steve asked.

Patsy just smiled.

"What do you think?" Michael said. There was a look of humor around his mouth.

Steve grinned. "Everyone's dream girl. Of course they listened to her."

"For the rest of the year," Sally reported, "that class was angelic. Mr. Gerstner thought he had died and gone to heaven."

"Adolescents can be horribly cruel," Patsy said. "They don't necessarily mean to be, but they often are."

"Patsy is never cruel," Michael said, "except to her boyfriends."

"I'm never cruel to anyone," Patsy said firmly. Michael looked amused but said nothing. Patsy felt an unfamiliar flash of annoyance. "Anyway," she continued crossly, "what do you know about my boyfriends?"

"Not much," he replied cheerfully, "except that you're cruel to them. Look at this Don fellow—cast off because he made the mistake of being petulant."

"Well, I don't see that I have to put up with all sorts of infantile behavior just because a man thinks he's in love with me."

"Of course you don't," Michael agreed.

Patsy's eyes actually flashed with temper.

"Haven't you ever been in love, Patsy?" Steve asked.

"She's always in love," Sally said. "The problem is it never lasts."

"That's true." For some reason Patsy began to feel depressed. "I don't know why, either."

"Your love affairs always conformed to whatever book you were reading at the time," Michael said unexpectedly. "When you were reading *Anna Karenina* you fell for Derek Forsyte, a Vronsky type if ever I saw one." Patsy stared at him in astonishment. "Then there was Peter Carteret when you were reading *Pride and Prejudice*."

There was a moment's silence. "Do you know," Patsy said in awed accents, "I believe you're right."

Sally and Steve rocked with laughter and Michael grinned.

Patsy thought of the book she had been reading

when she fell for Don. "But this is awful!" she said distressfully.

"Don't worry about it, Red," Michael said good-naturedly. "It's part of your charm."

Patsy straightened her shoulders. He sounded like her uncle, she thought indignantly. "Does the psychoanalysis come free or do you include it in your accounting fee?" she asked nastily.

He didn't seem to realize he'd been insulted. "It's free," he replied, looking directly at her. "Anytime."

The fluttery feeling was back in her stomach. His green-gold gaze held hers for a minute, then moved across the table to his sister's face. "How is Uncle Frank doing?" he asked, effectively dropping Patsy from his sight, his attention, and his conversation. Patsy stared at him in a mixture of outrage, bewilderment, and a new emotion she didn't quite yet recognize.

After dinner Michael and Sally huddled over the math problem Sally had mentioned earlier, and Steve switched on the TV. Patsy sat and watched with him, feeling ignored. It was a feeling she was totally unfamiliar with, and one she didn't like at all.

Before Steve drove him home, Michael asked Patsy if she would stop by his place in the morning before returning to New York. He had a few things to ask her about her tax records. Patsy opened her mouth to say no. But she said yes, instead.

Chapter Four

Sally's children were early risers—Patsy had Steven in bed with her at seven—and by nine o'clock the whole family was fed, and the grown-ups were showered and dressed.

"I'm going to rout Michael out," Patsy said to Sally. "I want to get back to New York by this afternoon."

"Okay," Sally said. "I just hope he didn't stay up all night working on that problem."

"Didn't you solve it last night?"

"Not completely. Frankly, I wasn't getting anywhere with it. Michael will, though." She made a rueful face at Patsy. "And *I'm* the one with the degree in higher mathematics. I'm also very smart. Michael, however, is a genius."

"He was always going to major in math," Patsy said slowly. "What made him switch to accounting?"

"Have another cup of coffee before you go?" Sally asked.

"Okay." Patsy sat at the kitchen table. The sun was shining in the windows and from the next room came the sound of the baby romping in his playpen. Steve had taken Steven with him to get the morning papers.

Sally poured the coffee and sat down as well. "It was my father," she said, "or at least, what happened to my father."

"I wondered."

"You remember how awful it was, Patsy? There was Daddy, president of his own engineering firm, respected, successful, and then—*bam*—bankruptcy. None of us had any idea that Cal Perkins had been embezzling from the firm. Or making those terrible investments. He was always good ole Cal, Daddy's trusted partner. Then Cal was in South America, and Daddy was left to face the music."

"Which he couldn't do," Patsy murmured sadly.

"No." Sally stared broodingly into her coffeecup. "The firm's collapse was bad enough. Daddy's suicide was"—she made a gesture—"unspeakable."

"I know," Patsy whispered.

"Michael couldn't get it out of his mind that Cal had gotten away with robbery like that for years. He couldn't believe that an audit hadn't picked it up. But Cal was clever, and evidently the auditor was not very thorough."

"Or as equally crooked," Patsy said.

"Or as equally crooked. Anyway, that was when Michael switched majors. Luckily, he had a wrestling scholarship, because there wasn't any family money left. I think it's kind of a crusade with him—to catch the crooks and protect the innocent."

"The incompetent nuisances with their affairs in a mess," Patsy quoted wryly.

"Precisely." Sally's thin, intelligent face was very serious. "He's not too popular in certain quarters, I'm afraid. He stirred up a nest of hornets when he caught Blanco."

"Mmm." Patsy stirred her coffee. "Who are his girlfriends?" she asked, completely changing the subject.

"There's been a succession," Sally replied, "but since college, he hasn't been serious about anyone. They've all been just—diversions." She sighed. "I wish he would get serious about someone. He should have his own kids, and not be spending all his paternal instincts on mine."

"Mmm," Patsy said again.

"You too." Sally eyed her friend. "It's time you stopped living like a butterfly and started thinking of settling down. You adore children."

"Like Michael, I have yours."

"Well, I'm not going to nag. I know you have a fairy-tale life and make millions of dollars, but I also know the real *you*, the person behind that incredible beauty of yours." She rested her chin on her hands and looked thoughtfully at said incredibly beautiful face. "I know we were teasing you last night, Patsy, but hasn't there ever been anyone you wanted to marry?"

"No," Patsy admitted regretfully. "There have been men I thought I was in love with, but to be honest, I never had any urge to marry. Which is funny, when you think of it, because I *do* want to get married; I *do* want children. But it has to be the right man, and so far . . ." She made a helpless gesture with her hands.

"I know. I was so lucky to find Steve. Without him, the world wouldn't make sense—if you know what I mean."

"Yes," Patsy said. "I do."

"I used to wonder sometimes what it must be like to be you, to live inside such a flawless body. Everything always seemed so easy for you. Anything you wanted, you got—with just a smile. The whole world was always in love with Patsy Clark."

Patsy's brown eyes were somber. She brushed a stray golden-red curl off her forehead and said, "It isn't always good to get things too easily."

"I suppose not. I said that to Michael once, you know, about wondering what it must be like to be you."

"Oh? And what did he say?"

"He said a very strange thing—a very perceptive thing, I think. He said that great beauty can sometimes be a burden, that a great many people will never get beyond the beauty, will be so affected by it that they'll totally fail to find the person underneath. He said it must often be difficult to be that person underneath."

There was a brief silence, and then Patsy said "That *was* a rather perceptive comment." Even to herself her voice sounded odd. She pushed her coffeecup away and rose. "Well, Sal, thanks so much for the hospitality, but I'd better be pushing on."

"Okay," Sally said equably. "Do you want me to ring Michael and tell him you're on the way?"

"That might be a good idea. I don't want to rout him out of bed."

"Will do," Sally promised and walked Patsy to her car. It was nine-thirty when Patsy pulled out of the driveway and started across the island toward the south shore and Michael Melville.

Michael was renting a house in East Hampstead, and at precisely five minutes after ten, Patsy rang his front doorbell. Receiving no answer, she rang again. His car was parked in the driveway, so she knew he must be home. She was just preparing to ring again when she heard a voice saying, "Okay, okay, I'm coming," and the door opened.

Michael stood in the doorway, wallet in hand. He was wearing a bathrobe over his pajama bottoms. His hair was tousled and he was unshaven. His feet were bare. He stared at Patsy. "I thought you were the paperboy collecting."

"I'm not," she answered helpfully.

"No, I can see that." He rubbed his head. "Sorry, the doorbell woke me up."

"Didn't Sally call to say I was on my way?"

"No."

"Oh she must have gotten sidetracked." There was a pause before she added, "Do you keep all your clients hanging about on the doorstep like this?"

"Sorry," he muttered, and held the door open wider. "Come on in. What time is it?"

"Ten o'clock. It's easy to see there are no children in this house."

They were standing together in the hall, he rubbed his head again and yawned. "I was up half the night with that damn math problem."

"Hmmm. Do you always look this ghastly in the morning?"

At that he grinned. "Come into the kitchen. I need a cup of coffee."

"Several, I should think," Patsy murmured. She followed him into an old-fashioned kitchen and watched as he assembled the coffee things. "I'll make it," she offered. "Why don't you go shower?"

A piece of his hair was standing straight up and she suddenly recalled the way he had looked as a little boy. "Good idea," he said. He smiled faintly. "I'll even shave."

He didn't look ghastly at all, Patsy thought. In fact, his rumpled, tousled, half-naked state was rather disturbingly attractive. Good God, Patsy thought, as she realized where her thoughts were leading her. This is Michael! Sally's little brother! What on earth has gotten into me? She marched to the percolator with determination and began to measure the coffee. Behind her, she heard him leave the room and go upstairs.

She was sitting at the scarred wooden table with a cup in front of her when he returned to the kitchen. His black hair was wet from the shower, and he was wearing an old pair of jeans and a plaid sport shirt with the sleeves rolled up. He went to the counter, poured himself a cup of coffee, and sat across from Patsy.

"What time did Steven have you up this morning?" he asked.

"He arrived in my bed at seven sharp. To keep me company, he said. Mommy had Daddy, after all, and he was afraid I was lonely."

He grinned. "What a diabolically clever excuse for getting into bed with a girl. I must remember it."

Patsy gave him an austere look. "Would you like me to scramble you some eggs?"

"Great." He sipped his coffee as Patsy collected eggs from the refrigerator and broke them into a bowl. He put the news on the radio, and they both listened while she cooked. When the weather report came on, Michael turned the volume up slightly. As Patsy placed a plate of scrambled eggs and toast in front of him, he gave her an absent-minded smile and picked up his fork, his attention clearly on the weatherman and not on her. Strangely enough, Patsy did not feel annoyed. At the moment she felt only contentment in waiting on him, and she sat across from him again and watched him eat. When the weather report was over, he switched the radio off and looked at her.

"The eggs are good, Red."

Patsy felt an absurd glow of pleasure at his words. Her lips curved a little and she took a bite of the toast she had made for herself. "Did you solve it?" she asked.

"The math problem? Yeah. At three this morning."

Patsy finished her toast and, putting her elbows on the table, rested her chin on her hands and regarded him gravely. Her gaze didn't appear to disturb him at all. He finished his coffee, wiped his mouth on a napkin, and said, "Come into my study and we'll take a look at those taxes."

His study was off the kitchen in what would have been the dining room in a more conventional household. It was furnished with a huge desk, which was covered with a great number of tidily arranged papers, and several walls of bookshelves. Looking around, Michael realized there was no chair for Patsy and went out to the kitchen to get her one. He set it down in front of the desk and then went around to the chair behind it. He picked up a piece of paper and sat for a minute in silence, frowning thoughtfully.

Patsy felt a twinge of alarm. "There isn't anything wrong, is there."

He looked up. "On the face of things, no. The cash receipts books and the bank statements seem okay."

"Seem? What is this 'seem'?"

"Well, I haven't done any checking yet."

"What kind of checking?"

"Checking that the checks written down in the cash books were really issued to the company indicated and in the amount stated, for one thing."

Patsy frowned. "But why on earth wouldn't they be?"

"They wouldn't be if Zimmerman was ripping you off, sweetheart, and pocketing huge amounts of the cash he said he was buying you things like shopping-center shares with."

"What a rotten thing to say! Poor Fred isn't even in his grave yet."

"I'm not saying he's a crook, Patsy. For all I know, the guy is pure as the driven snow. But I won't know for sure until I do some checking."

Patsy glared. "You have a nasty, suspicious mind."

"Mmm." He looked preoccupied. There was a faint line between his well-marked black brows. "I'm an accountant. I'm always suspicious."

Patsy remembered what had happened to his father. "Well, go ahead and check," she said in a gentler voice. "But the IRS wants to see me next week."

"I talked to Maginnis Thursday afternoon. He's given you an extension."

"You never told me that!"

The line between his brows smoothed out. "I just did," he said. "Now, you tell me this . . ."

After ten minutes of relentlessly thorough questioning, Patsy was feeling a bit limp.

"I hope the hell this Zimmerman is honest, sweetheart," Michael said grimly, "because you are a sitting duck."

Patsy bit her lip. "But, Michael, I paid Fred just so that I wouldn't have to bother about things like contracts and investments and taxes and so forth."

"A sitting duck," he repeated.

"You *know* how wretched I always was in math." She looked a little subdued and very beautiful as she sat there in her pleated linen pants and matching oatmeal linen jacket. Her skin was flawless in the merciless morning light.

He smiled crookedly. "I know." He put the papers he had been looking at back on their proper pile. "Well, all right, I'll do some checking and let you know how things stand."

Once again he was dismissing her. Patsy found that she did not want to be dismissed. She looked out the window. "The weather is beautiful," she remarked. "You have a perfect day for whatever it is you're planning to do."

He raised an eyebrow. "How do you know I'm planning anything?"

"You were glued to the weather forecast," she pointed out.

"I guess I was." He moved his shoulders a little as if he felt a sudden cramp. "I just thought I'd go to the beach for the afternoon if the weather was good. Blow some of the cobwebs out of the brain."

Patsy had a sudden vision of a stretch of empty white sand, silent but for the sound of gulls and of waves crashing against the jetties. "The beach," she repeated. "That sounds marvelous." She looked at him. "Do you mind if I come too?"

"In that outfit?"

She looked down at her very expensive silk blouse and linen pants. "Why not?"

He grinned. "Why not, indeed?"

They were not quite the only ones on the beach when they arrived nearly forty-five minutes later. There was a group of teenagers playing Frisbee, and a young family whose children were digging industriously in the sand. Michael and Patsy walked along the waterline. Michael wore sneakers and Patsy was barefoot—she had left her fashionable shoes in Michael's car. She had left her jacket as well and was wearing a sweatshirt of Michael's over her silk blouse. They strolled for a while in silence and then Michael said, "How can anyone live out of reach of the ocean?"

Patsy looked up at him in surprise. "I was just thinking the same thing."

He smiled a little. "Those kids back there reminded me of us."

"I know. We went from digging sandcastles, to playing Frisbee, to picnics after the prom. Really, when you think of it, half our childhood was spent on the beach."

"Mmm. One of these days I'm going to buy a beach house. With a big porch so I can look out at the water first thing in the morning and last thing before I go to bed at night."

"That sounds lovely," Patsy said dreamily. She inhaled deeply. "The smell of the salt. There's nothing like it."

"Remember the time your father took us all fishing out of Freeport?" he asked.

Patsy started to laugh. "Do I ever! Sally was the only one who wasn't sick."

He chuckled. "First you'd heave over the side, then me, then you . . ."

"Poor Daddy."

"And Sally, the stinker, kept on catching fish after fish."

They had come to one of the jetties, and Patsy rested on a flat rock. It was warm from the sun. She looked up at him as he stood over her. "I guess we're creatures of the land."

"I guess so." He sat down next to her, his shoulder almost touching hers.

"It doesn't seem so long ago, does it?" she asked softly. "And yet it's vanished—that world of our childhood. Mother and Daddy are in Arizona, your folks are dead, the houses are sold." She looked up. He was very close to her.

"You sound awfully melancholy." His eyes were on the ocean; his profile looked set and stern.

On impulse she rested her face against his shoulder. She could feel the hardness of muscle under her cheek. She closed her eyes. "I feel melancholy," she murmured.

There was silence and after a minute she opened her eyes. He was looking down at her, an inscrutable expression in his eyes. "You are a menace, do you know that?" he said.

Patsy sat up. "A menace?"

"Unquestionably."

She stared. "What do you mean?" She recognized the expression in his eyes now—it was amusement. "Stop looking so smug," she said tartly. "I don't know what you're talking about."

"I know you don't. You've always gotten off perfectly unscathed, with no idea of the wreckage you've left behind."

"You sound like the Delphic Oracle. Are you naturally like this or do you like being enigmatic?" Her voice was too obviously calm.

He grinned and stood up. "Come on. I came here for a walk, not to sit around on rocks being lazy." He started down the beach and Patsy had to break into a jog to catch up with him. It didn't occur to her that this was probably the first time in her life that she had ever chased after a man.

"What do you mean, 'wreckage'?" she asked after they had walked in silence for a while. She glanced at him swiftly and saw the corners of his smile. "I don't go for married men, I'll have you know," she added self-righteously.

"I never thought you did. It's not something you can help, Red. It's just the way you are. Wherever you go and whatever you do, there'll always be some poor bastard breaking his heart over you."

Patsy stared straight ahead. "I can't help the way I look."

He chuckled. "No, I suppose you can't."

She put her hands into her pockets and scuffled sand with her feet as she walked. "Well, at any rate I never broke *your* heart," she said a little defiantly.

"Of course you did." Her head snapped up in surprise and she turned to stare at him. "Me and every other boy at Central High," he went on imperturbably. "How we dreamed about you. How bleak you made our futures seem. No other girl seemed worth our attention when there was Patsy Clark, shimmering before us like a heavenly garden of forbidden fruit." He shook his head in mock sorrow. "We learned early what it was to know the heartache of lost dreams. You made the rest of our lives seem like second best."

There was a long pause. "Are you *serious*?" Patsy asked in astonishment.

"Perfectly serious." He smiled reminiscently. "God, how I lusted after you when I was fifteen." His mouth wore a faint, nostalgic smile and there was amusement in his eyes. It was as if an older and wiser man were looking back on the follies of his misguided youth.

Patsy was suddenly extremely annoyed. "You're being ridiculous," she said crossly.

"Not ridiculous," he corrected her. "I was being fifteen."

"And now you've grown up and know better."

"*I* do," he said peacefully. "But what about poor Don?"

"The hell with Don," Patsy snapped, and lengthened her stride, moving ahead of him. Behind her, she heard a distinct chuckle. It was not a sound that improved her temper.

When he bestirred himself to catch up with her, however, he didn't pursue the subject that had angered her so, but began to talk about something quite different. By the time they returned to his car, Patsy's naturally sunny disposition had resurfaced. They sang with the radio all the way back to Michael's house.

Chapter Five

Monday Patsy went to her first filming of a TV commercial for a camera company that had signed her to endorse its products. Contracts with big companies to represent them in advertising campaigns was the surest sign of success in modeling. They did not come along too often, and this was Patsy's biggest contract since her sports-clothes endorsement.

She knew the makeup artist, the director, and the cameraman from other sessions. They all got along well and the filming went smoothly.

"It's a pleasure to work with you, darling," the director told her as the session broke up at about six. "You're a professional."

Patsy laughed. "I've been doing this long enough, Doug. I feel like an old lady these days. The last magazine I looked through was filled with pictures of fifteen-year-olds."

"I know. They burn out, though, darling. Five, six months and they're finished."

She frowned slightly. "I know. Why is that?"

"They get spoiled, get that tough, bitchy look," Mark the makeup man, answered. "The companies hire the kids because they want a fresh, dewy look for their products, and once a girl loses that look she's finished. You can't fix that hardness with makeup." He looked at Patsy. "*You've* still got the freshness," he said. "You can still look better than kids twelve years younger than you."

"Thanks," Patsy said. "I think."

Mark, who knew her well, smiled. "The biggest difference between you and the kids is very simple, darling. You're *nice*."

Patsy wrinkled her nose. "I was older when I came into the job," she said. "And I had parents who kept my feet very firmly grounded. The rags-to-riches bit is just too much for most of these kids. They can't handle it. You ought to have more patience, Mark. They're really rather pathetic."

"They're a pain in the ass," Doug said rudely. "And Mark is right, darling, you are nice. I hope you last for ten more years."

"Hah," Patsy said. "In two years I'll be thirty. I've already lasted longer than most." She smiled. "But it's been fun. See you, guys." She walked out of the studio, knowing they were watching her. What she didn't know was that the emotion reflected in their eyes was one of pure affection.

It had been a long, tiring day, and Patsy was stretched out on the sofa with her feet propped up when the phone rang. She went into the bedroom and picked it up.

"Hello, Miss Clark?" inquired an unknown voice.

"Yes." Patsy's number was unlisted and she didn't often get calls from people she didn't know. She frowned now, afraid she was once again hearing from the IRS.

"I'm Bob Hellman, Miss Clark, a friend of Fred Zimmerman's. Fred asked me to take over for him when he had his heart attack."

"Oh," Patsy said. This must be the man whose name Fred had wanted to give her. "Well, it's very good of you to call," she said kindly, "but I've already gotten someone to look after my financial matters."

There was a moment of curiously charged silence on the other end of the line. Bob Hellman's voice, when he spoke, sounded pleasant, however. "Oh, have you? That's too bad. I was looking forward to working for you. And Fred filled me in on a few of the things he was doing. Would it be at all possible for me to discuss my credentials with you?"

"I'm really sorry, Mr. Hellman, but I have definitely engaged someone else."

"Well, so be it," he said genially. "Would you mind telling me who beat me out?"

One of the things Patsy had learned in the course of a very public career was to volunteer as little information about her private life as possible. "Yes," she said. "I would mind. It was kind of Fred to be concerned about me, and kind of you to call, Mr. Hellman. Have a pleasant evening."

Patsy hung up and thought no more about Bob Hellman. In fact, her mind seemed to be running rather disconcertingly on quite another accountant, but her thoughts were not finance-oriented. Michael hadn't even suggested that she stay when they had returned to his house from the beach yesterday. In fact, she had gotten the impression that he was anxious to get rid of her. She had assumed, with a gloom that was unusual for her, that he probably had a date.

Patsy had ended up spending Sunday evening with Don. It was one thing to say Don had to go, but quite another, it seemed, to convince him of that fact. She couldn't blame him, really. They had been going together for over a year, and at one time Patsy had fancied herself quite in love with him. He was a successful news reporter, clever, intense, and a bit of a rebel. Things had been terrific for the first six months: they liked the same things, they were good in bed, they had the same kind of humor. Then he wanted them to move in together. Patsy had had a few serious boyfriends in the years since she had moved to New York, but she had never formally lived with anyone. She loved her parents too much to cause them that kind of upset.

She told him she wouldn't live with him, and then, when he began to pressure her to marry him, she knew she didn't really love him, after all. She had known that for quite some time, actually, but had been trying to hide the knowledge from herself. It depressed her unutterably, the way she always seemed to fall out of love.

She thought about that gloomy fact now as she fixed herself an omelette and salad for dinner. "I'm just a shallow, fickle person, I suppose," she said out loud. She sat at the kitchen table to eat, her mouth drooping tragically. Halfway through the omelette she began to feel better; she'd had scarcely a thing to eat all day. She was cleaning up the kitchen when the phone rang again.

It was Sally. "Someone at the hospital gave Steve four tickets for opening day at the stadium," she informed Patsy immediately. "Steve is a miserable Met fan, but he knows what fanatic Yankees his wife and brother-in-law are, so he took them. Do you want to come too?"

"Is Michael going?"

"Are you kidding? Michael would cancel an appointment with the president for the Yankees. Of course he's going. You used to be a pretty red-hot fan yourself, I remember."

"I still am," Patsy said instantly. "I'd love to go."

"It's Thursday afternoon."

Patsy mentally canceled a lunch with a movie agent. "Fine."

They made arrangements to meet at the stadium and Patsy hung up. Her mood of depression had quite vanished and she went to bed in a decidedly cheerful frame of mind.

The weather was perfect for opening day. Steve had been given tickets for one of the boxes, and Sally and Michael were in heaven.

"I can't believe you grew up on Long Island," Steve grumbled good-naturedly as he listened to his wife. "Long Islanders are supposed to root for the Mets."

"Anyone who knew Mr. Melville rooted for the Yankees," Patsy informed him kindly. "It was a matter of sheer survival."

Michael, who had been looking around the stadium, turned to his brother-in-law and grinned. "The Mets stink," he said simply.

"They have some good, young talent this year," Steve defended his team loyally. "I think they'll do all right."

The public-address system crackled and then the announcer boomed out a welcome to the fans. The stadium was quite filled for a midweek afternoon, and Patsy found herself smiling with pleasure. All four of them were wearing slacks and sweaters. The men had taken their jackets off, but Sally and Patsy still wore theirs. The April sun was warm but there was a spring chill in the air.

"I haven't been to a ballgame since high school," Patsy said in surprise.

The visiting team was being introduced and Michael turned to her. "You probably haven't been to one since Dad took us all for Sally's sixteenth birthday."

"You're right. That's the last time I was here." She looked around as well. "It's changed."

"Here they come!" Sally cheered, and seconds later the announcer started to introduce the home team.

"Batting first and playing second base," the loudspeaker boomed, "Joe Hutchinson." They all applauded vigorously and Michael threw in a whistle for good measure. The second and third batters were introduced and then came the announcement the whole stadium was waiting for.

"Batting fourth and playing center field," the announcer shouted, and the spectators rose as one to their feet, "*Rick Montoya!*"

Sally shrieked, Patsy shouted, and Michael let out a sort of yodel that Patsy instantly recognized from bygone days. The ballplayer they were all so loudly saluting jogged onto the field, tipped his cap, and then flashed his famous grin at the fans. They yelled back louder than before.

"The guy hasn't even swung his bat yet," Steve said.

Michael sat down. "Watching Montoya swing a bat is sheer poetry," he remarked to Steve. "Even the Mets might win if they had him in their lineup."

"And he's so *gorgeous*," Sally added. "I think he was smiling right at us."

"Were you applauding his skill or his pulchritude?" her husband asked.

Sally grinned. "Both."

"I need a beer," Steve said, and Patsy giggled.

It had been a perfect day, Patsy thought two hours later as the game moved into the ninth inning. She had forgotten what vociferous fans the Melvilles were. She had forgotten, too, what tremendous fun a baseball game could be.

"Good God," Sally mumbled a little acidly, "here comes the TV camera again. I've been afraid to blow my nose all afternoon."

"The camera is not focusing on you, Sal," her brother said unkindly.

Sally stared at him, affronted, and Steve put an arm around her shoulder. "That's all right, Babe. Patsy may have a TV camera following her about like a shadow, but what does she know of the binomial theorem?"

"Not a damn thing," Patsy answered cheerfully.

"A beautiful thing, the binomial theorem," Michael put in. "Sheer poetry."

"It is not," Patsy said positively. "Wordsworth is poetry. And Yeats. Not the biniminal theory—or Rick Montoya's swing, either."

Michael winced as if in acute pain. "Binomial, Patsy. Not biniminal."

"Whatever," Patsy said sunnily, and smiled. It was her best smile, the one that usually reduced men to quivering jellies at her feet.

Michael said blandly, "The camera is thataway," and went back to watching the game.

Patsy stared at his faintly hawklike profile and inwardly fumed. He had been much nicer when he was younger, she thought.

The Yankee pitcher retired three men in a row in the the top of the ninth and the game was over, the Yankees winning three to one. As they left their seats, Michael and Sally absorbingly discussed the team's prospects for the coming season, while Patsy and Steve walked behind them, chatting casually.

"Where did you park your car?" Steve asked Patsy as they reached the sidewalk.

"Nowhere," Patsy replied. "I took a cab."

"A cab?" Steve frowned. "You're never going to find another taxi in this crowd."

Sally had overheard the last part of this exchange. "We'd run you home, Patsy, but I promised the baby-sitter we'd be back before six. If we delay any longer, we're going to hit the rush."

"That's okay, Sally. If I can't find a cab, there's always the subway."

"The *subway*," Steve said darkly. Like all suburbanites he held the view that the subways were only slightly less dangerous than Beirut under siege.

Michael laughed. "Not everyone who rides the subway is inevitably raped or murdered," he said to his brother-in-law. "However, to soothe your jangled nerves, I will drive Patsy home."

"So chivalrous," murmured Patsy, who hadn't taken her car precisely because she wanted things to fall out this way.

"Sometimes I even astonish myself," he replied. "Come on, my car is this way." After a round of thanks and promises to call soon, Patsy left the Maxwells and followed Michael to the lot where he had left his car.

Traffic around the stadium was heavy and it took them quite a long time to get out of the Bronx and into Manhattan. Michael didn't say much; he had turned on the radio and appeared to be listening to the music. Patsy rested her head against her seat and watched him drive. His car had a standard shift and he let the clutch in and out automatically, changing gears with easy competence, his mind clearly on something else.

"When you traveled," he said abruptly, "who made your arrangements—plane fare, hotels, so forth?"

She stirred slightly. "Fred, of course."

"You went on vacation last year to Africa?"

"Yes. To the Serengeti game preserve. Then I spent some time in Egypt."

"Mmm. And Fred made all the arrangements?"

"Yes." Her brown eyes looked troubled. "Why are you asking me this, Michael?"

He changed the subject. "Do you have a bank account in the Cayman Islands?"

"Of course not!" She was beginning to sound impatient. "Why on earth should I have an account there? I've never even *been* to the Cayman Islands."

"The Cayman Islands operate a banking system not unlike Switzerland's." His voice was expressionless. "No names are used—only numbers. You can stash quite a lot of money in a numbered bank account, and there's no way the IRS will know it's there. You're supposed to report the account, of course, but very few do."

"Well, I don't have an account like that," she repeated.

"When I went to Zimmerman's office the other night, I cleaned out all his files pertaining to you. One of the things I found was a bank book from the Cayman Islands."

"In my name? Oh, no, you just explained there was no name." Patsy pushed a stray piece of hair off her forehead. "Well, then, the bankbook must have been Fred's."

"Yes," Michael said in that same expressionless tone. "That's what I figured." He stopped at a light and turned to find her regarding him worriedly. He smiled. "I don't want to drive home in this traffic, and I owe you a dinner. Is there a restaurant where we can go dressed like this?"

Patsy's brow smoothed out. "Of course. Luigi's. The best Italian food in New York."

"Luigi's. How original."

"That's really the owner's name," Patsy said serenely. "And wait until you taste his cooking."

Luigi was always thrilled to see Patsy, and he put forth his best efforts in her behalf. It was almost nine when she and Michael left the restaurant, and they had done a lot of filling in of those seven years during which they hadn't seen each other.

They walked slowly along the sidewalk toward her apartment, still talking easily.

"Come up for a nightcap?" she offered as they reached the car, which her doorman had parked in front of her building for them.

Every other man Patsy knew would have jumped at the invitation; Michael merely shook his head. "Thanks, but I'd better be getting home. I'll have to work twice as hard tomorrow for taking the afternoon off today."

"I suppose you will," Patsy said a little forlornly.

They had stopped next to his car, and Michael reached up and tilted her face toward the glow of a streetlamp. She looked at him, acutely aware of his strong, slender fingers lying so lightly on the curve of her jaw.

"I have theater tickets for tomorrow night," he said softly, "and, like you, I recently broke up with the person I've been going with." His eyes were half-hidden by his lashes. "Would you like to go?"

"Yes," Patsy answered instantly.

She could see him clearly in the light, but she could not read the expression in his narrowed green-gold eyes. A faint smile touched his mouth. "They're for *The Real Thing*," he said.

"Great. I haven't seen it yet."

The pressure of his fingers on her jaw increased infinitesimally. He bent his head and kissed her, casually and gently. "I'll pick you up at seven-fifteen," he said, and turning away, unlocked his car door.

The doorman of her building, who had been an interested witness to the scene, moved forward, and Patsy turned to him. "Good evening, Howard," she said. "Thanks for parking the car for us. However do you always manage to find a spot right in front of the building?"

Chapter Six

Patsy had her delayed lunch with the movie agent on Friday and then did some shopping. At Saks she bought a lovely spring-green silk dress by Bill Blass and a new pair of evening sandals with heels lower than those she usually wore. She went home, showered, had a light supper, and put on the new dress. She brushed her hair away from her face and high up on the back of her head, with just a few ringlets falling artistically along the white slenderness of her neck. When she had finished, she surveyed herself in the mirror. The slim bodice and waist of the dress fit her perfectly and the full, soft skirt fell gracefully to just below her knees. Patsy thought with satisfaction of the luck that had made her a perfect size eight and went into the living room to wait for Michael.

He was on time and they decided to leave his car with Howard and take a cab to the theater. Michael's tickets were for the third row in the mezzanine.

Patsy draped her lightweight coat around the

back of her seat and sat down, calmly ignoring the stares she was provoking from all sides.

"Sorry it's not the orchestra," Michael murmured into her ear.

"Don't be smug," she returned imperturbably, and he gave her a quick sideways grin. He was wearing the same light-gray suit she had seen on him the other day, and she thought he looked extremely handsome.

The play was wonderful, both funny and thoughtful, and the acting was superb. They decided to walk to Sardi's for an after-theater drink and snack, and as they strolled down Shubert Alley, Michael commented on the quality of the performance.

"I know," Patsy returned. "Seeing Jeremy Irons and Glenn Close like that only confirms my determination to stay a million miles away from the movies."

"Have you had offers?" Michael asked curiously.

"Not exactly, but I've had plenty of agents who swore they could find me a role and could launch me on a whole new career. I had lunch with one this afternoon, in fact. He couldn't believe I wasn't interested."

"Why aren't you?"

"Simple," she replied. "I can't act."

"That hasn't stopped Marly Andrews," he murmued.

She grinned appreciatively. "Yes, well I hate making a fool of myself. And think how scandalized

Mother would be. I saw this guy this afternoon only because he was a friend of Fred's."

"Ah," he said, "Fred."

They had reached Sardi's and the maître d' proved very accommodating, finding them a table even though the restaurant was crowded. They ordered drinks and Patsy said she didn't want anything to eat.

"Are you sure?" Michael asked. "I'm going to eat. I only grabbed a quick sandwich for supper—I worked until after six."

"You go ahead," Patsy replied. "I never eat this late at night. It's the worst possible thing you can do—the weight just pours on while you sleep."

He looked at the spring-green size eight sitting so gracefully across the table from him. "Do you have to worry?"

"I make sure I don't have to worry," she said firmly. "I eat three sensible meals a day and at the proper hours. I absolutely loathe dieting. It's much easier not to have to."

"Makes sense, I guess."

"Besides," Patsy said truthfully, "I'm not hungry."

"Well, okay. But I'm going to have the biggest cheeseburger they can make."

While he ordered, Patsy sipped her white wine slowly, and when he turned back to her, she made an obvious attempt to brighten up.

"What's the matter, Red?" he asked softly. "You've been downcast ever since we left the theater."

She forced a smile. "Sorry. I didn't mean to be a wet blanket."

"What's bothering you?" he repeated. "Was it the play?"

She sighed. "Yes. It hit too close to home, I guess." She looked into her glass and slowly moved the wine back and forth. "I guess I saw a little of myself in Annie," she said, still looking at her drink, "and I can't say I liked what I saw." He didn't answer, and she looked up to find him watching her gravely. "You know that scene at the beginning, when she tells her husband she's in love with Henry and she's leaving him? And then, when the husband falls to pieces, all she can think of is that his distress is in such bad *taste*?" He nodded, still not speaking. "Well," she continued unhappily, "it reminded me of Don and me. I broke up with him Sunday, you see, and he made the most ghastly scene. The thing was, he really meant it. He did care. And all I could think of was that his dramatics were in such bad taste. He made me feel guilty and uncomfortable, you see, and I just wished he would stop and go away." She pushed her drink toward the middle of the table and said tragically, "I'm a terrible person, Michael. I don't mean to be, but I am."

He smiled very faintly, although his eyes remained grave. "You're not a terrible person, Red."

She felt tears sting her eyes. "What's the matter with me?" she almost wailed. "I gave a year of my life to Don. I thought I loved him. And now I don't care if I ever see him again." She sniffed. "In fact, I hope I don't."

He handed her his handkerchief. "You made a mistake," he said matter-of-factly.

Patsy blew her nose. "It wouldn't be so bad if it were just Don," she continued, her voice muffled by his handkerchief. "Sally was teasing me about always being in love, and it's true. I do think I'm in love, and then it always turns out that I'm not. It's very depressing."

Michael's quick smile flashed. "I see," he said. And then he laughed.

"It isn't funny," Patsy said mournfully. "I want to feel about love the way Henry did in the play tonight. I want to find 'the real thing.' But I'm afraid I never will. I'm too shallow."

"The one thing you are not, sweetheart," he said comfortingly, "is shallow."

The waiter arrived with his cheeseburger and Michael ordered another round of drinks. Patsy watched him bite into his burger. "You don't think so?" she asked hopefully.

"Nope."

"Then what's the *matter* with me?" she repeated in genuine bewilderment.

"Not a thing in the world," he assured her. "Mmm, this is good. Want a french fry?"

"All right." Patsy reached out and snared one off his plate.

"You just haven't met the right guy yet," he said after he had swallowed. "You have a great capacity for love, Patsy, I'm quite sure of that. Up until now you've mistaken liking and sexual attraction for love—it's something that's very easy to do. The number of divorces proves that, I think."

"I guess so," Patsy said doubtfully.

"When you meet the right man, you'll know it."

Patsy took another french fry. "How can you be so sure?"

"Because it's a completely different feeling. When 'the real thing' hits, you'll know it, all right."

"Has it hit you?" Patsy asked very softly.

"Yep. So I know, you see. The other thing is just a diversion."

He knew. That meant . . . Patsy did not like to think of what it meant. "What happened?" she asked.

"She didn't love me," he replied simply, and took another bite of his cheeseburger.

"Oh, Michael." Patsy's great brown eyes were filled with compassion.

He smiled crookedly. "Don't look so tragic. I've learned to live with it."

"She's a fool," Patsy said abruptly, and he shook his head.

"No. She's a lot of things, but she's not a fool. Have another french fry?"

"If you insist," Patsy said, and helped herself.

His car was parked once again in front of her apartment. "Come up for a cup of tea," she said as they got out of the cab.

"I don't think—" he began.

"*Michael*!" she cut in, "I promise not to seduce

you. Now will you stop making excuses and just come up?"

She had succeeded in startling him, she saw. Taking his arm, she gave an impatient tug.

The familiar grin dawned. "Take back that promise and I'll come."

It was her turn to be startled. She decided to ignore his last comment. "Come on," she repeated, more softly this time, and he walked beside her into the building. They didn't talk until they were in her apartment.

"Do you want tea?" she asked him, "or another drink?"

"Tea please." He followed her into the kitchen and sat at the table while she got out the tea kettle. "All your Englishness comes out when you make tea," he remarked idly as he watched the deft movements of her hands.

"Well, Mother was born in Surrey," she replied. "And she never has become very American, not even after forty years."

He watched as she put cups and saucers on the table. "We both spent the afternoon with a friend of Fred's, it seems," he murmured as she sat across from him.

"Oh?" Her brows lifted. "Who did you see?"

"A fellow named Bob Hellman. He said you told him I was handling your business affairs. He tried to talk me into turning them over to him. I refused."

Patsy looked at him in confusion. "He told you I had given him your name?"

"Yes."

"Well, I didn't." The kettle began to whistle and she got up to make the tea.

"Hellman said he called you," Michael explained when she was sitting once again.

She poured the tea. "He did. And I told him someone else was handling my affairs. He asked who it was and I said I wouldn't tell him." She put the pot down. "I've learned to give out as little information as possible about my private life."

He was very still. Patsy looked at him gravely. "The ballgame," he said at last. "We were all over television together at the ballgame."

Patsy cleared her throat. "*I* have a famous face," she said.

He swore without apology. His mouth suddenly looked very hard in the bright kitchen light. He hadn't touched his tea.

"Michael," Patsy croaked from a dry throat, "will you please tell me what's going on?"

"Fred Zimmerman was ripping you off, for one thing," he said brutally. "That trip to Africa, for example. He charged you a lot more than it cost."

"But how—"

"Easy enough. Like all good swindles, he did it on paper. He has receipts for everything. The problem is, the receipts are a work of fiction. He charged you much more for plane fares, hotels, and guides than the airlines, hotels, or guides ever saw. The difference went to Fred—or rather to his numbered bank account in the Cayman Islands."

Patsy's eyes were huge. "Are you sure?"

"I'm sure, all right. I spent the whole day checking." He looked at her. "You're also paying five hundred dollars a month more for this apartment than it actually costs."

Patsy put her hand to her forehead. "I can't believe all this," she murmured dazedly.

"You can believe it all right, sweetheart. And I've only just started checking. You were quite a little gold mine for Fred."

Patsy stared at her tea. "But he was always so *nice* to me."

"So should I have been if I were in his shoes."

Patsy's head remained bent, the loose ringlets bright golden red against the soft white skin of her neck. "Oh, Fred," she said with infinite sadness.

"Oh, Fred, indeed." Michael's voice was hard, and his eyes, when she looked up, were impatient and ruthless. "The question now is, Who is Fred's pal and how did he get my name?"

Patsy stared at him as if she'd never seen him before. He didn't look at all like the Michael she knew—or thought she knew. And at the moment he didn't look like anyone she'd care to tangle with. "I don't know," she said in a small voice.

"Neither do I." The grimness around his mouth didn't relax. "But I have a distinctly unpleasant feeling that I'm going to find out shortly."

"Your tea will get cold," she said helplessly. He picked up the cup and drank. His eyes were hooded, unreadable.

She tried to change the subject. "I'm going to be on the island tomorrow. Ebony Lad has been shipped to Aqueduct from Florida and he's running his first race. As part owner, I get the pleasure of sending him off."

She had his full attention. "Did Fred recommend that horse to you?"

"Yes."

"I'll come with you to the track."

"Well, all right."

"Why don't you drive to my house first and we can go to Aqueduct together?"

"All right," she repeated.

"What time?"

"About noon?"

He nodded decisively. "Okay. Noon." He stood up. "Thanks for the tea."

Dismissed again, she thought. She stood up as well. "I haven't been bossed around so much since I was a little kid," she complained.

He looked around, really seeing her for the first time since the subject of Bob Hellman had come up. She was standing by the refrigerator, and she gave him a slow and beautiful smile. Her dark-brown eyes were huge, and they held his for a long, silent moment.

He crossed the kitchen and stood before her. "You don't need a boss, Red," he said softly. "You need a keeper." He put both hands on the refrigerator behind her, imprisoning yet not touching her. His face was very close to hers and she felt every pulse in her body leap with awareness.

Her lips parted very slightly. "Are you applying for the job?"

He smiled faintly, and Patsy stopped breathing. "I think I've already got it, sweetheart," he said. He straightened up and moved away from her. "I'll see you tomorrow at noon."

Patsy straightened her own shoulders and glared at him.

The smile lingered on his mouth. "Remember your promise," he said.

"Good night," she answered coolly. "Please close the front door after you."

"And you make sure it's locked. See you tomorrow." He was gone. Patsy listened to the sound of the door closing and abruptly sat down. She could not remember ever being so confused by a man in her life.

Chapter Seven

Patsy rang Michael's doorbell at twelve-fifteen the following day, and they set off immediately for Aqueduct in Michael's car. He did the driving.

"It's not a big-stakes race or anything," Patsy explained as they cruised along the highway. "Earl said it was a warm-up, a race to get him used to the track and give him a bit of a workout against the other horses."

"Do you often watch him run?"

"I go to all his races in New York. He really is a love, Michael. Wait till you see him. He has the most beautiful face."

Michael spared her a glance from the road. "When did you acquire this interest in horses?"

"I've always liked horses. I read all the Black Stallion books when I was a kid. But Mother would never hear of my taking riding lessons, so I sort of got interested in other things."

"I thought the English were crazy about horses," he remarked.

"Mother had a younger sister who was killed by a

fall from a horse." Patsy's voice was full of compassion. "Everytime I mentioned riding, her face would get this frozen, petrified look. I hated to see her upset, so I gave it up." She rolled down her window a little to let the breeze blow into the car. "Anyway, when Fred mentioned that a racehorse might be a good tax shelter, I remembered all those Black Stallion books and said go ahead."

"You said you were part owner?"

"Yes. I own half, in fact. The other half is owned by another fellow Fred worked for, a guy named Frank Carbone. He seems nice enough."

"So did Fred," he said dryly.

Patsy sighed. "True."

They parked the car and went to the barn area of the track where Ebony Lad was stabled with the rest of the horses trained by Earl Hibbard. The trainer was nowhere in sight, but one of the grooms came over to them. "Lad's looking good, Miss Clark," he told her. "Would you like me to take him out of his stall for you?"

Patsy smiled. "Would you, Tim? I'd like Mr. Melville to see him close up."

"Sure." The groomed lifted a halter from the door, went into the stall, and buckled it around the horse's head. He clipped a lead line on the halter and led the horse into the April sun.

He was a big, strong colt who was just coming into his full growth. He wore a light blanket, but the coat on his neck gleamed pure black in the sun. "Isn't he marvelous?" Patsy asked proudly. She went to the horse's head and reached into the pocket of her cord pants for a piece of carrot she had brought. The horse's ears pricked forward and he nuzzled her, impatient for his treat.

"He sure is big," Michael said.

"Just over seventeen hands," the groom informed him.

Patsy had finished feeding Ebony Lad his carrot and was gently stroking his nose. "You're a big boy, aren't you, fella?" she crooned gently, and at the sound of her voice, the horse's ears pricked forward again.

"Patsy!" said a genial male voice, and a small, stout man with thinning blond hair appeared from around the corner of the barn.

"Hi, Earl," Patsy greeted him cheerfully. "I'd like you to meet a friend of mine. Michael Melville—Earl Hibbard."

The ruddy face of the trainer wore a pleasant expression. He held out his hand. "Glad to meet you."

"I've just been admiring your horse," Michael said easily. "He's very quiet, isn't he?" Ebony Lad was once again nuzzling Patsy's pocket.

"What he is, is greedy," Patsy said producing another carrot.

They remained for a few minutes longer, the three of them chatting in the sun, and then Patsy's eye caught an approaching pair of men. "Here comes Lad's Daddy," she remarked to Michael. "Hi, Frank. Are you here to give him a royal sendoff?"

The man she was addressing was tall, slim, and

dark-haired. He gave her a very white-toothed smile. "I'm glad to see you, Patsy. How are you?"

"Fine." She glanced around for Michael, who, standing beside Ebony Lad's head, was hidden from the view of the newcomers. "Frank, I'd like you to meet a friend of mine," Patsy began, and Michael stepped out from behind the shelter of the horse. Frank and his companion saw him at the same second and their expressions froze. Patsy's voice faltered momentarily and then went on evenly, "Michael Melville. Michael, this is Frank Carbone."

Frank nodded, and so did Michael. Neither man made a motion to shake hands, nor did Frank offer to introduce his friend. It was the friend, Patsy noticed, who was staring hardest at Michael. He did not look friendly.

"How do you do," Patsy said graciously to the unfriendly one. "I'm Patsy Clark."

The heavy-jowled, well-tanned, mean-looking face turned briefly in her direction. "Yeah," he grunted. "I know."

Patsy allowed her eyes to widen, and she looked at Frank. "Is this gentleman a friend of yours?"

"A business associate," he replied.

"Oh?" Patsy turned to Michael, who appeared to be engaged in a staring contest with the business associate. Michael looked perfectly self-contained and rather frighteningly tough.

As Patsy watched, the hazel eyes removed themselves from the baleful dark stare of Frank's friend and focused on her. "Shall we move along to the clubhouse?" he asked her.

"Yes," she replied. "We might as well take in some of the races."

"Mmm." He put his hands into his pockets. "I have a feeling that this might be my lucky day."

The expression on the business associate's face hardened from unfriendliness into menace. Michael looked at Patsy, and she fell into step beside him immediately.

"Whew!" she said as they moved out of earshot of the men. "Who was *that*?"

"That, my dear Patsy, was a man I almost put in jail."

"In jail!" Patsy echoed in astonishment.

"Yep. He was engaged in some extremely crooked dealings which I picked up on a tax audit. But he had a very smart lawyer, and friends in high places, I also suspect. He got off on a technicality." Michael's black hair was blowing over his forehead in the breeze. "He doesn't like me."

"I'll say he doesn't. And why, I want to know, is a crook like that a business associate of Frank's?"

"The plot thickens." He sounded rather pleased. Patsy stared at him. "And at least we know now how Bob Hellman got my name."

"You think Bob Hellman's connected with— what's the business associate's name, anyway?"

"Jack Garfield. And, yes. I think Hellman is connected. They all appear to have been buddies of the sainted Fred."

"Oh, dear," Patsy moaned. "Poor Fred."

"Sweetheart," he said, "I think rather it's a case of poor Patsy. Do you realize that Fred had control of all your money?"

"Yes," Patsy replied rather hollowly. "I've been realizing that for the last day or so, Michael."

"You stand to lose quite a bundle."

"So I've gathered." She linked her arm in his. "We'll have to try to recoup my fortune at the races." She looked into his face. "Who do you like in the first?"

Ebony Lad won his race in impressive style and Patsy succeeded in banishing the thought of Frank and his unpleasant friend from her mind. They stayed for the last race, which Michael won, cashed in his ticket, and claimed their car.

"Can I buy you dinner before you set off for home?" he asked as they got on the expressway.

"You certainly can. You can afford to, the way you cleaned up this afternoon."

"Mmm. I didn't do badly at all. I'll have to try this horse-racing business again." Someone cut him off and he frowned slightly and hit the brakes. Patsy thought he was absolutely the most imperturbable person she had ever met. "Seafood okay?" he asked.

She started a little. "What?"

"I asked if you'd care to eat seafood. For dinner."

"Oh, yes. Seafood would be fine."

They went to a small, unpretentious restaurant near the beach and had clams, shrimp, and a bottle of white wine. It was about eight o'clock when

Michael parked in front of his house. Patsy's Volvo was in the driveway. They got out of the car, and he gave her a friendly smile. "Got your keys?" he asked.

Patsy stared at him. "It's awfully early. You might offer me a drink before you kick me out onto the highway."

"Mmm," he said. "Well, come on in, then."

Hardly a gracious invitation, Patsy thought as she followed him down the path. Really, she didn't know why she was tagging after him like this. Pique, probably, she decided. She wasn't used to being dumped.

Michael switched on the living-room lights. "I have ginger ale or Diet Seven-Up," he said.

Patsy rested in a club chair. "Do you have Scotch?"

"Yep. For me, not for you. You're driving and you already had a few glasses of wine."

"Oh, all right," Patsy grumbled. She took her feet out of her espadrilles and wiggled her stockinged toes comfortably. "Seven-Up then."

He went into the kitchen and returned with a tall glass for her and a short one for himself. Then he sat on the sofa. "About these shopping-center shares," he began.

Damn the shopping-center shares, Patsy thought crossly. Was accounting all he ever thought about? She sipped her Seven-Up and looked at him speculatively. There was a folder on the coffee table in front of him and he leaned forward to open it.

"Is that my stuff?" she asked.

"Yes."

He turned a paper over and Patsy suddenly got up and went to sit beside him. She put her drink on the table and bent forward, so that her head was close to his. A silky strand of red hair tickled his cheek. "Show me," she said softly.

"Patsy . . ." There was an odd note in his voice and she turned to look at him. The green-gold eyes held a distinctly wary expression. She moved a bit closer, her breast brushing against his arm.

"Yes?" she said, her voice even softer than before.

His hair had fallen forward over his forehead. "My dark-eyed siren," he said, eyeing her with the same wariness but now also, she could swear, with amusement. "Are you by any chance trying to seduce me?"

Her brown eyes widened slightly as the idea registered. She didn't really know what she was trying to do. She sat back a little as a whirl of thoughts raced through her brain.

Patsy did not make a habit of seducing men. Her moral standards might not conform to those of her mother, but she could say, with perfect truth, that she had never gone to bed with a man she didn't love. Her boyfriends had always been long-term, never spur-of-the-moment impulses. So what was she trying to do now?

The answer came immediately. She was trying to get him to pay some attention to her. Her pride was irked by his indifference, that was all. She suddenly felt ashamed of herself. Good God, she thought, this was Michael. He was practically her brother, for heaven's sake. "No, I'm not," she said, and bent forward to give him the kind of kiss he had once given her—light, casual, sisterly.

He put his hand on her arm and kissed her back, and this time his kiss wasn't brotherly at all. In seconds Patsy, having completely lost the initiative, found herself leaning back against the sofa cushions with Michael above her. When he finally raised his head, she was trembling.

"Because if you are," he added, and the eyes looking down into hers were pure gold, "I'm perfectly willing."

"Michael." It was barely a thread of sound. She had never felt quite like this before; it was as if all the supports had been knocked from beneath her. She could get away now, she thought. She could laugh, make a joke, and everything would go back to the way it had been. Her eyes didn't move from the serious intensity of his face. There was a deep nocturnal silence in the house, as if they were the only two people in the world. She didn't say anything more, and he bent his head to kiss her again. Patsy's arms reached up and encircled his neck. When his mouth finally left hers and moved slowly down her throat, she bent her head back for him. He kissed the hollow of her throat and undid the first button on her blouse.

"You have such beautiful skin, Red," he murmured. He undid another button and then another, his mouth following where his hands led. Patsy made no move to stop him. She lay back

against the sofa pillow and very slowly buried her
hands, caressingly, in his hair. The blouse fell away
from her body, his hands moved again, this time to
unhook her bra. He kissed the white curve of her
breast. "Like silk," he said.

"Oh," she whispered and at the ragged little
sound, he lifted his head and looked at her.

There was desire in his eyes—hard, burning,
intense. It was a look Patsy was familiar with, and
usually it had given her a feeling of power. It had
been rather satisfying to know one could reduce a
man to this. Strange that her feelings should now
be so different. She felt weak before that look in
Michael's eyes; she wanted to succumb to him, to
please him, to let him please her.

"No?" he asked with a note of controlled inquiry.

Patsy gazed at him. With those hazel eyes and
high-bridged nose he looked like a falcon, she
thought, a beautiful, merciless falcon. She was suddenly afraid. This was different, she realized. This
was different from anything she had ever known
before. His question hung poised in the air between
them for several seconds, before Patsy, with huge
dark eyes and slightly parted lips, very slowly,
nodded her head yes. His eyes narrowed to slits of
gold. "Let's go upstairs," he said.

Patsy's knees felt weak when she stood, and she
negotiated the stairs with difficulty. She didn't
understand what was happening to her, but she did
understand she was powerless before it. They
reached the second floor.

"This way," Michael said, and effortlessly picked

her up, carried her into a room, and laid her down on a bed. He bent to kiss her again and, while doing so, competently finished undressing her. Then he stood, pulled his crew-neck sweater off, and tossed it onto a chair. "I'm glad you decided to stay for a drink," he said. He had finished unbuttoning his shirt, and it followed the sweater.

Patsy watched him. Beyond him, near the window, a small lamp was lit on a dresser. A moth had gotten in and was battering around under the shade. With a part of her mind, Patsy was aware of the small, violent, futile battle of the moth, and then Michael was beside her, the bed squeaking a little as it took the brunt of his weight.

Patsy had been right. It was different from anything she had known before. It was passionate and intensely sensual and soul-shatteringly sweet. It left her feeling as if she would do anything in the world for him, and being Patsy, she kissed his shoulder and told him so.

He put an arm around her and drew her close. "You might try a repeat of what you just did," he replied easily. He wasn't as unruffled as he sounded, however. Patsy was close enough to feel the still-hurried beat of his heart. He felt warm, strong, and comfortable beside her, and her eyes closed in contentment. Above her head his voice took on a tinge of amusement. "Though not, perhaps, just yet."

Patsy snuggled her head into the nook of his shoulder. "I'm glad you're letting me stay," she murmured.

His fingers buried themselves in the silky tangle of her hair and moved caressingly. Patsy sighed with pleasure. "You can stay, Red," and the amusement was quite gone from his voice. "You can stay as long as you like."

"Good," Patsy mumbled drowsily. "I will." And she drifted off to sleep in the comforting shelter of his arm.

He woke her up at seven the following morning and she did, indeed, give him the repeat performance he had requested. Afterward they lay together, drowsy and content, with the sunshine streaming in between the slats of the blinds. The bedroom, Patsy noticed, was sparsely furnished. There was a big chest of drawers that someone had antiqued a Williamsburg blue; the bed, which was only a frame, spring, and mattress; an end table laden with books; and a straight-back chair, which was now heaped with their clothes.

"Do you rent this house furnished?" she asked lazily.

"No. The classy furniture you see is all mine."

"Hmm. I see you thoughtfully provided yourself with a double bed."

He laughed deep in his throat. "One likes to be prepared for any goodies that might come one's way."

"Wretch," Patsy said, but her thoughts were not as pleasant as her voice. Was that all she was—a "goodie" who had come his way? Well, she asked herself severely, what else should you be? You practically begged him to make love to you, and even after he had as much as told you he still loved someone else.

The sound of the doorbell interrupted her thoughts.

Michael swore softly. "Collecting for the paper," he said, and got out of bed.

"Let him come back another time." Patsy yawned.

"Have a heart." He had pulled a pair of jeans out of the closet. "I'm never home. The poor kid could spend his life trying to collect from me." He went to the door, his bare torso dappled with sunlight as he passed the window. "I was a paperboy once myself," he said, and left the room, closing the door behind him.

Patsy snuggled under the covers. The minutes passed. Surely it shouldn't take this long to pay the paperboy, Patsy thought. From downstairs there came the distinct sound of something breaking. Patsy jumped out of bed and ran to the closet to find Michael's bathrobe. She wrapped it around herself firmly and went out the door and halfway down the stairs, where she stopped and looked into the living room.

There was a tremendous fight going on between Michael and two men. Patsy stared for a moment in horror at the writhing bodies and flying fists and then announced, loudly and clearly, "I've just phoned the police. They said a patrol car was in the area and would be right here."

The fight subsided somewhat as the two strangers turned at the sound of her voice. "Let's get the hell out of here," one of them yelled.

"The door," Patsy pointed out helpfully, "is open."

They fled. Patsy continued down the stairs and closed and locked the door behind them. Then she turned to Michael.

He had gotten to his feet. There was blood on his face and on his shoulder. "Good for you, Red," he said.

"Are you all right?" She could feel herself starting to shake with reaction. "You're bleeding. What was that all about?"

"Did you really call the police?" he asked.

"No."

He grinned. The blood ran heavily from a cut over his eyebrow. He looked genuinely pleased. "That's my girl."

Patsy felt her breath falter, and she inhaled deeply. "Come along and let me attend to your face," she said, and obediently, he followed her into the kitchen. He sat on a wooden chair while she got a clean towel and tried to staunch the blood.

"I presume those thugs were friends of the business associate," she said flatly.

"Um." She was pressing his head back against her breast as she held the towel to his eyebrow. He closed his eyes.

"Why didn't you shout for help?"

His long lashes never flickered. "I thought I was giving them as good as I got."

"It was two against one," Patsy said and he smiled faintly. Her lips set in an unusually grim line. "What did they want?"

"To scare me off," he answered peacefully. "Bully tactics."

"And you don't scare off easily," she answered slowly.

He let the whole weight of his head rest against her breast. "Well," he said. "I can be a bully myself, if I have to be."

Patsy removed the towel and looked closely at the cut. "It might need stitches."

"You patch it up, Red. You're good at that sort of thing."

Patsy frowned. "Where are your bandages?"

"Upstairs, in the medicine chest."

"All right. Here, hold this towel firmly in place. The cut's still bleeding."

Patsy fetched the tape and gauze and placed a makeshift butterfly bandage over the wound.

"You would've been a good nurse," Michael told her when she had finished.

"Sometimes I'm sorry I let myself get sidetracked away from it." She went to the sink and washed her hands. "I was all set to start nursing school, you know, and I thought I might earn some money during the summer by modeling. It was a lark more than anything else. I just walked into the Marks Modeling agency two weeks after graduation and asked if I might possibly be a candidate for a job."

"And they thought you might."

She dried her hands and turned to face him. "At first I thought I'd delay nursing school for a year, but instead of fizzling out, as so many modeling careers do, the jobs kept coming. The money was great, and it was fun, so" —she shrugged her slim, graceful shoulders—"here I am."

"Here you are," he agreed. "And though you're not a nurse, you do make a great pot of coffee. How about it?"

Patsy gazed at him assessingly. His face looked tan against the white bandage. The cut on his shoulder had been only superficial. Without his shirt, the muscles in those shoulders and arms were very evident. He was right. He had been giving them as good as he got.

"Coffee it is," she said. "Are you hungry?"

"Just toast, please."

"Okay."

"I'm going to give Sally a call," he said as she got out the coffeepot. "I want to store all your files at her house. Would you mind driving?"

For a minute, as she measured coffee into the percolator, she didn't answer. Then she turned and said carefully, "Michael, I don't like this one little bit."

"No need to worry, Red," he said soothingly. "Just a precaution."

She stared at him, and her brown eyes were troubled. "I don't want you to get hurt."

"I won't be." He sounded reassuringly firm. "Make the coffee."

She turned back to the stove. "Why do you want me to drive?"

"Well," he said cheerfully, "I think I may have a small concussion."

Patsy closed her eyes. "I'll drive," she managed to say calmly, and finished measuring the coffee with a not-quite-steady hand.

Chapter Eight

❧

Patsy and Michael ate a light breakfast and showered, then Patsy helped Michael load her car with the cartons containing her files.

"You don't have any other plans for today?" Michael asked belatedly, after the last carton had been stashed in the back seat.

"No."

He merely nodded. "Then let's get started."

"All right. Maybe my hair will finish drying in the car." She had washed her hair in his shower and the ends were starting to feather a brilliant golden-red as they dried. "I never heard of anyone who didn't own a blow-dryer," she added, with mock exasperation.

"Well, now you have." He looked a little preoccupied. "Just think of how I'm broadening your horizons."

"Yes," Patsy said dryly. "Get in the car."

The long lashes lifted, his eyes looked very green this morning, she noticed. "Yes, ma'am," he drawled, and opened the door.

The drive to Sally's was quiet. Patsy kept surreptitiously checking Michael out of the corner of her eye. If he looked as if he were drowsing off, she was going to detour straight to the nearest emergency room. He stayed awake, however, and his color looked reasonably good. As she pulled into Sally's driveway, he said, "Satisfied?"

She put the parking brake on. "What do you mean?"

"You've been watching me like a mother hen for the whole ride."

She took the key out of the ignition and turned to face him. "A concussion can be serious," she said severely.

He didn't answer, only laughed and opened his car door. "Hi, Sal," he said to his sister, who had come out to greet them. "Thanks for the loan of your basement."

Michael and Steve carried the cartons to the basement, with Steven excitedly following them up and down, up and down. When they had finished, Steve asked Michael, "How about a game of one on one? We just put up a basketball hoop."

Sally gave Patsy an ironic look. "For Steven," she murmured. "Of course, it will be at least four years until Steven can reach the basket, but . . ."

"Michael got bashed on the head this morning," Patsy put in very firmly. "He's not going to play basketball, Steve."

A faint smile flickered across Michael's face. He

turned to his brother-in-law. "So pretty," he said regretfully, "and so bossy."

"How did you get bashed on the head?" Sally asked in her best big-sister voice.

Steve took a small pencil-light out of his pocket and shone it into Michael's eyes. "Look to the right," he said. "Now left. Now over my shoulder." Steve put the light back into his pocket and touched the back of Michael's head. Michael winced. Steve frowned. "That's some lump, fella."

"That's also some bandage over your eye," Sally commented. "For God's sake, Michael, what happened?"

"Yeah." Steve frowned harder. "And why do you need to store Patsy's files in our basement?"

"Didn't you tell them?" Patsy asked Michael incredulously.

"Er, no."

"Tell us what?" Sally demanded.

"Fred was involved with a gang of crooks and he's swindled me out of a fortune," Patsy answered succinctly.

"Crudely put, perhaps, but essentially correct," murmured her accountant.

"*What!*" Sally shrieked.

"Crooks?" Steve said.

"Sit down," Michael replied resignedly, "and I'll tell you."

The story took some time, after which Sally fixed them lunch. Then, because the sun was shining and Steve so obviously was longing to play with his new toy, Patsy took pity on him. "I'll play you a game of basketball," she offered.

"You?" Steve asked with scarcely flattering incredulity.

Michael and Sally exchanged a glance. "Good idea, Patsy," Sally said. "He needs a challenge."

Steve made an obvious effort to be polite. "Okay, Patsy, if you want to."

"Mommy is terrible," Steven added helpfully. "She always misses."

"Come and watch Aunt Patsy, honey," Sally said with a smile. "She's better than Mommy."

"I don't know if I am," Patsy murmured as they all went out to the driveway. "I haven't shot a basketball in years."

"I'll park the car in the street," Michael volunteered, and as he backed out of the driveway, Patsy practiced a few lay-ups.

"Not bad," Steve was saying kindly as Michael returned.

"I played in high school but not much since," Patsy said. She dribbled the ball down the drive, turned, and sank a jump shot. Steve's eyes widened. "No rough stuff under the basket," Patsy warned as she walked back to him. "You're bigger and I'm playing in espadrilles."

"Well, that should even the odds," Sally said wickedly.

Steve turned to look at his wife. "I think I'm being set up."

Sally grinned. "Patsy was high scorer in the county for two years in a row. Michael"—she turned to her brother—"get a couple of beach chairs out of the garage so we can watch in comfort."

The game quickly became hilarious, with Michael rooting for Steve and Sally egging on Patsy. Steven, joining the male club, loudly encouraged his father. The game ended when Patsy missed a ten-footer and Steve rebounded and sank the ball. He won by two points.

Sally made lemonade, and Steve was a magnanimous winner. "You have a terrific shot," he complimented Patsy. "I had no idea you played ball."

"If she'd only been more aggressive, she could've been the tops," Sally said. "You were always too nice, Patsy."

"Mother always thought basketball was terribly unladylike," Patsy said.

The telephone rang, and Steve went to answer it. He returned shortly and spoke to Michael. "It's for you. Your partner, Ted Lawson."

Michael raised a black eyebrow, excused himself, and went into the house. When he reappeared his face was expressionless—so expressionless that Patsy knew something was wrong.

"The office has been broken into," he told them. "Ted stopped by to pick up something and found the door had been forced and the files rifled." He looked at Patsy. "We'd better go over there now."

She rose to her feet and answered quietly, "Okay."

"Broken into!" Sally cried. "Michael, do you

think it's those creeps who beat you up this morning?"

"It's certainly a possibility."

Steve looked worried. "This is a tough crowd you've gotten yourself mixed up with, Mike."

"Yeah," Michael said.

Sally kissed him. "Be careful." She turned to Patsy. "Are you going to be safe?"

"Of course," Patsy calmly assured her. "Don't worry, Sally." Then she said to Michael, still in the same tone, "I'll drive."

"Okay." They went to the car, waved reassuringly to the worried faces of Sally and Steve, and started down the street.

"Do you think they were looking for my stuff?" Patsy asked.

"Yes."

Patsy bit her lip. "I'm so sorry I landed you with this mess, Michael. I had no idea . . ." Her voice trailed off.

"I'm not sorry." He looked relaxed and composed, and Patsy found herself wondering just what it would take to smash that seemingly invincible self-command. He smiled a little and changed the subject. "It was nice of you to let Steve win."

Her lips curved. "Steven was watching, and I didn't care."

"I know. If you had cared you could've been great."

"I don't know." Michael had cared, she thought as she drove along the crowded highway. He had chosen wrestling for his sport and he had gone at it with such single-minded determination that he had been state champion by his junior year. They were such different types of people. She knew nothing of the determined intensity that characterized him. She had never gone after anything in her life. She drifted, she thought dismally, floated along happily on the lucky combination of genes that had produced her face. What a shallow person she was, she thought again unhappily, and sighed.

"Don't worry, Red," Michael said from beside her. "It'll be okay."

He spoke soothingly, almost automatically, in the sort of voice one would use to comfort a frightened child. If she hadn't been driving, Patsy thought with a twinge of exasperation, he probably would have patted her. "I certainly hope so," she returned a little tartly. "I never realized accounting was such an exciting profession."

"It has its moments."

"So it seems." Patsy turned off the highway onto the exit. "Do I make a right here?"

"Yes."

Ted Lawson was waiting for them at the office, along with the police. All of the file cabinets had been gone through and the ones in Michael's office had been emptied and strewn all over the place.

"Do you have any idea who might have done this, Mr. Melville?" the police officer asked.

"Not offhand," Michael said neutrally.

Patsy's eyes widened. "You're not working on anything that would show up an embezzler or something like that?" querried the other officer.

"From the looks of things here, I quite probably am," Michael replied. "I won't be able to tell you what case, though, until I see if anything is missing."

The policeman asked him another question, and Patsy stood and listened in growing astonishment. He wasn't going to tell them anything—not that he had been attacked that morning; not that he had taken her files to his sister's; not anything. She was absolutely thunderstruck.

He talked professionally to the policemen. Then, after the squad car had gone, he talked soothingly to his partner. Finally Ted Lawson left as well, and Michael turned to Patsy, who had been unusually silent the whole time. "Let's get out of here," he said. "I'll cope with the mess in the morning."

She didn't move. "Why didn't you tell them?"

He looked at her, his eyes hooded. "This isn't a case for the local gendarmes, Patsy."

"And just who is it a case for, then?"

"The federal authorities. Eventually."

"I see. Eventually."

"Yeah. First I want to check out those shopping centers Fred invested in so heavily."

"*You* want to check them out?"

He put a competent arm around her shoulders. "Come on, Red. We're both tired."

Patsy walked with him to the door. "You're not the Lone Ranger," she said.

He patted her. "I know."

When they got to the car, he opened the passenger door for her. "I'll drive this time."

He was treating her as if she were a mental incompetent, Patsy thought mutinously as she got into the car. And he *was* acting like the Lone Ranger.

Michael's house was quiet when they arrived, but when he put his key in the front door to unlock it, he found the door already open. He grunted in surprise and stepped back.

Patsy's heart plummeted into her stomach. "You locked that when we left," she said.

"I know I did. Go out to the car, Patsy. Lock the doors. If I don't come out in two minutes, call the police."

Patsy's mouth was so dry she wasn't sure if she could speak. "Michael . . ." she managed.

"Go ahead." He spoke gently but firmly, and she found herself returning to the car. As soon as he saw her lean over to lock the car door, he went into the house.

He was back out in less than a minute, gesturing for her to join him. She jumped out of the car and ran up the path. "They didn't just search the office," he said grimly. She shot him a quick look and went into the living room.

The house was a shambles. Failing to find what they wanted, the intruders had done as much damage as they could. Patsy stared in horror at the wreckage around her. "Oh, my God," she whispered.

"Yes." His voice was expressionless but his eyes were terrifyingly cold. "Upstairs is just as bad."

"The *bastards*," Patsy said passionately. "They

didn't have to do this. This was more than searching for some papers."

"This was bully tactics, sweetheart."

"I'm going to call the police," she said decisively, but he reached out and grabbed her arm.

"No police. Not yet."

"But, Michael . . ."

He was slowly shaking his head. "They're trying to scare me, Patsy. Your files are important, true, but the IRS has a lot of the same material. It's not the files they want so much as they want me to back off the case."

"Well, then," she said reasonably, "why don't we just turn everything over to the IRS and let them handle it?"

His eyes traveled slowly around the room. "Do you know, Red, I'd rather wait a bit. Perhaps we can save something for you out of the mess."

"Michael," she said earnestly. "I don't care about the money. Please, let's go to the IRS."

He said the same thing to that idea he had said to calling the police. "Not yet."

"But, why?"

His eyes narrowed. "Let's just say I have a little score to even up with the bully boys."

Quite suddenly all the stress of the day came to a head and Patsy lost her temper. "Men!" she said furiously. "You're all the same—one step out of the cave. You positively *enjoy* bullying and bashing each other about. All you require of a woman is that she be a good-enough nurse to patch you up so you can start bashing all over again. And that she be availa-

ble in bed in case you want a little sex, of course."
She was glaring at him now in outraged indignation.

He had begun to smile when she launched into her speech, and as she finished, his face broke into a wide grin. "Sounds like a good program to me," he said. "Especially that last part."

Patsy stared at him and tried to hold on to her anger, but it dissipated as quickly as it had come. "Stay with me for a while," she said abruptly. "You can't stay here in this mess." She looked around with horror. "Half the furniture is broken." And you'll be a lot safer in my apartment, guarded by plenty of security personnel and three locks, than you will be in this very vulnerable house, she thought to herself in the brief silence that followed her words.

He was looking at her, his face grave. "Are you serious?"

"Perfectly serious. You can't stay here. Michael, *please*." She hoped the panic she was feeling did not show in her voice. If he stayed here and those thugs came back. . .

"You could twist my arm," he said.

"Consider it twisted. Pack a suitcase and I'll try to straighten out the kitchen while I wait."

They left the house two hours later and stopped for dinner before crossing the bridge into Manhattan. They took Patsy's car and left Michael's parked in his garage.

"Mr. Melville will be staying with me for a while,

Howard," she told the doorman. "And nobody else at all is to be allowed up to my apartment. Under no circumstances. Is that clear?"

"Yes, Miss Clark." The doorman hastily concealed his surprised expression. "Good evening, sir," he said to Michael.

"Good evening," replied Michael, and he and Patsy went upstairs. She unlocked the three dead bolts, and he entered, carrying his suitcase.

Patsy switched on the living-room lamps and closed the drapes against the darkness. Michael sat on the sofa and stretched his legs in front of him. "This is much nicer than my place," he said.

"I'd hardly call that a compliment," Patsy murmured dryly. "Tea?"

"Mmm. Tea sounds good."

He stayed in the living room while she went to the kitchen to put the kettle on. She arranged the tea things on a tray and then walked quietly back down the hall to the living room.

He was still sitting on the sofa where she had left him, idly leafing through a magazine from the coffee table. His black hair was rumpled and untidy and he needed a shave. She paused for a moment in the doorway, her eyes on his partially concealed face. He looked tired, she thought. The room was very quiet, and suddenly it seemed to Patsy as if time had abruptly stopped. There was no movement in the room, just the sight of Michael sitting on her sofa reading a magazine. The very blood and breath in her seemed to still. Then he raised his eyes and saw her. Patsy's heart gave one loud thump and then began to race uncontrollably. He was looking at her inquiringly, and for one endless moment she couldn't speak.

"Tea ready?"

"Almost." She was speaking, but her voice sounded strange to her own ears. "Do you take sugar?" she forced herself to say. "I forgot."

"No, no sugar. Just milk."

The kettle began to whistle and she fled thankfully back to the kitchen.

It had happened. After all these years, it had finally happened—the one, the only, the forever love had finally come into her life. And she was too late. He loved someone else.

She made the tea with unsteady hands. It was Michael himself who had told her she would recognize real love when it came her way. "When you meet the right guy, you'll know it," he had said. He was right. It was a completely different feeling from anything she had known before. Patsy stared at the tea tray. What am I going to do? she thought in forlorn bewilderment.

"Do you need some help?" It was Michael, coming into the kitchen.

Patsy jumped. "Oh," she said, "Er, yes. You could carry this tray into the living room for me."

"Sure." He lifted the tray and started down the hall.

Patsy followed, breathing deeply and trying to get her nerves under control.

Chapter Nine

❦

They had their tea in the living room, and Patsy managed to summon up most of her usual poise. She wouldn't worry about the future, she thought as she drank her tea, watching Michael's face and listening to the even tones of his voice. He was here with her now; that's what mattered. She would take whatever the present had to offer and leave the future to take care of itself. Patsy had always had the happy facility of living for the moment.

Michael put his teacup on the coffee table and stretched.

"You can use the closet in the spare room," Patsy said. "And there should be a few empty drawers in the dresser." She stood up. "Bring your suitcase and I'll see what's available."

She had some coats stored in the spare-room closet, but there was still plenty of room. And two drawers in the dresser were indeed empty. Michael put his suitcase on one of the twin beds and turned to her.

Patsy was standing between him and the door,

and in the muted glow from the bedside lamp, her face looked incredibly beautiful. The soft light cast shadows in the hollows of her cheeks and accented the high cheekbones and huge, dark eyes. Her blouse was open at the neck and the line of her throat was exquisite. "You can sleep in here if you like," she said softly, "but you might feel less lonely with me."

An odd silence fell between them. He looked taut as a drawn bow, she thought. All his usual easy repose was gone. She crossed the room and stood before him. "Michael?" she said cautiously and she tentatively reached out and put her hand on his arm.

His reaction was instant, automatic, inevitable. With his other hand he pulled her to him and his mouth came down to cover hers. His kiss was hard and hungry, and Patsy melted into him, giving herself up to it completely. Finally he raised his head, and she looked through her lashes at the face that was so close to her own. What she saw there set the blood racing through her veins. "Darling," she breathed, "come inside."

He didn't answer but followed her into her bedroom. The lamp on the desk was lit, and the room looked warm, honey-colored, and very feminine in the soft light. Patsy kicked off her shoes and let her feet sink into the deep carpet. Lifting her big brown eyes to his, she raised her hands and began to unbutton her blouse. It slipped off her shoulders and onto the floor, followed by her lacy white bra. Her golden-red hair hung loose on the pearllike skin of her bare shoulders. Her breasts were pink-tipped and perfect, her eyes very dark, her cheeks exquisitely flushed. She reached out and began to unbutton his shirt.

He was standing very still, but when she touched him, she felt him tremble. He wanted her; that much was certainly clear. So why did she sense this mysterious resistance in him? It was another woman, she thought, the woman he loved, trying to come between them. I won't let her, Patsy thought fiercely. I'll make him forget her. She finished unbuttoning his shirt and slid her arms under it, around his waist, so that her breasts pressed against his bare chest.

"Love me, Michael," she whispered, a seductive, impossibly beautiful enchantress, and under her hands he shuddered. "Love me," she repeated, and his hands caressed her bare back, drawing her closer. She felt the hard muscles of his body under her fingers, felt the aching, drowning passion of his kiss. Then she was lying on the bed and he was kissing her throat and her breasts. His beard stubble scratched her sensitive skin. He put his mouth on one pink nipple and the breath caught raggedly in Patsy's throat. He unbuttoned her slacks and she raised her hips so he could draw them off unimpeded. She was on fire, and when he paused momentarily to rid himself of the last of his clothes, she lay, helpless and quivering, aching for him to return to her. And when he did, he continued his erotic exploration of her body until they both knew, at the very same second, that it was *now*.

For a moment, as Michael was poised above her, Patsy was aware of the smooth sheet under her back, of the little hiss of the radiator as heat came up to take the chill off the spring evening. Then he was in her, and her body opened to him, moved to him, as the shocks of pleasure ripped through her again and again.

When finally he lifted his weight off her, she slowly and reluctantly opened her eyes. She was afraid. She heard the ticking of her old-fashioned clock in the silence of the room. There was never again going to be anything like this in her life and she knew it. But did he? What could she expect from him, who loved someone else?

Next to her Michael very softly said her name, and she turned and buried her face in his shoulder. His arms encircled her, holding her, cradling her with infinite gentleness, infinite tenderness. And Patsy felt safe and comforted, and her fear was gone.

When she awoke early the following morning, he wasn't there. She sat up abruptly, then heard the sound of the shower. Slowly she slid back down and gazed dreamily at the ceiling. The shower was turned off and she heard movement in the spare room. Drawers were being opened and closed. He was getting dressed. She looked at the clock on her night table; it was six.

When finally he came into her room, he was dressed in a blue pin-striped suit. "You're certainly an early bird," she said, she hoped with composure.

His thin, serious face lit with its wonderful smile. "I have a gigantic mess to deal with at work, remember?" He was crossing the room toward her bed. "And a stack of clients whom I've been neglecting in the cause of one Patricia Clark."

"I'm afraid I can't say I'm sorry," she whispered. She could drown just looking into his eyes, she thought.

He bent over and kissed her, gently, lingeringly. "Would you like to get up and make me breakfast?" he murmured against her mouth.

"Darling," she breathed, "I'd love to."

He straightened up and watched her get out of bed and walk to the closet. She pulled out a green silk robe and slipped it over her nakedness. She tied it firmly at the waist, then turned, her hair tumbling about her face and shoulders. The green silk hung softly about her tall slenderness and the smile she gave him was both sleepy and sensuous.

"Do you know," he said softly, "that you are enough to drive a man mad?"

Patsy looked at him, feeling the power of him, the force, all the way across the room. She smiled again, this time with mischief. "Would you like to show me?"

"I'd love to." A faint, answering glimmer danced in his hazel eyes. "But I can't. Not now, at any rate. I have to get to work."

Patsy sighed. "All right. Come out to the kitchen and I'll feed you."

The early-morning sun was pouring into the kitchen, and as Patsy made bacon, eggs, and coffee, she felt perfectly happy. He was sitting at her table, eating her cooking, and tonight he would be coming home to her. She put some toast in front of him, kissed the still-damp top of his head, and sat across the table from him.

"What are you planning to do today?" he asked.

"They're doing some new layouts on the sportswear I endorse, so I have a modeling session at eight-thirty."

He put his coffeecup down. "Where are these clothes advertised?"

"They do circulars, Michael."

"Who is 'they'?"

"The manufacturing company."

"Mmmm. Do you have any of these circulars?"

"I'm sure there are some around here somewhere," she replied vaguely.

He looked mildly exasperated. "Red, you are the worst businesswoman I have ever met."

She looked gloomy. "I know, I know. Brains are not my forte."

"I didn't say that. I said business was not your forte." She looked at him a little doubtfully. "You used to write some damn good poetry, if I remember correctly," he continued.

She flushed. "That was high-school stuff."

"I remember it as being very good." He finished his eggs. "I always thought you had a very good brain," he said, and astonished, Patsy stared at him. He grinned. "It just doesn't work logically."

"Wretch," she replied good-humoredly.

He stood up. "Find me those circulars, sweet-heart. And I need your car."

"I know. You have the keys anyway." She followed him to the door. "When will you be home?" she asked, and thought, What a nice ring that has. Home.

"I don't know. Probably not until late. I'll call you."

"Okay. And, Michael . . . be careful."

"Yes, Miss Kitty," he drawled, and she laughed. He kissed her briefly and then was gone.

Patsy heaved a huge, tremulous sigh and went to take a shower.

Most of the shooting crew was at the studio when Patsy arrived. The morning session went smoothly, and it was only when they broke for lunch that Patsy noticed the man standing behind the lights. He came over to her. "Hi, Patsy," he said amiably. It was Frank Carbone, co-owner of Ebony Lad. Patsy's heart dropped into her stomach.

"Hi, Frank," she answered in natural surprise. "What are you doing here?"

"Waiting for you. Look, Patsy, I have to talk to you."

She smiled sunnily. "Great. You can buy me lunch."

He smiled back and Patsy thought with unchar-acteristic cattiness that he looked like a movie star in a B film. "I'd love to," he replied, and she left the studio with him, hoping her shaking knees were not obvious.

They went to a restaurant on the next block. "A drink?" he asked as they sat.

Patsy never drank while she was on a job, but she thought she could use something at the moment. "I'll have a glass of white wine," she answered. She looked around idly, and behind the beautiful mask of her face, her brain was working furiously. How had Frank known where to find her? Her agent never gave out her whereabouts.

The drinks were served, and Patsy took a long sip of hers. "So, Frank," she said gaily, "how did you find me?"

"I called your agent," he replied absently, and Patsy's heart thumped. "I have to talk to you, Patsy, about Michael Melville."

"About Michael?" She put her drink down to hide her trembling hands.

"Yeah. He's not a good guy for you to get mixed up with."

Patsy managed a very credible laugh. "Good heavens, Frank," she said lightly. "Michael and I grew up together. I've known him almost since I was born. Whatever can you mean?"

His handsome face looked suddenly heavy. "I mean you should dump him off your account, Patsy."

She let her eyes widen in indignation. "I most certainly will not! And I don't see what business it is of yours anyway."

"It's my business because I like you, Patsy." This time there was no mistaking the menace in his voice. "I'd hate to see that pretty face get ruined."

He looked like a snake, Patsy thought. A nasty, creepy, cold-eyed snake. She could feel herself grow white under his stare. "Are you threatening me, Frank?" she asked a little shakily.

"Not threatening, beautiful, advising." He smiled. "Like I said before, Patsy, I like you."

"I'm honored." She stood up. "Good-bye, Frank," she said coldly, and turned to leave.

He stood up quickly and grabbed her arm. She stayed perfectly still, restraining with difficulty a strong urge to scream. "Have you listened to what I've been saying?" he asked.

"Yes." Her face was stony.

"And?"

"And I like Michael much more than I like you, Frank. You or your business associates." She jerked her arm out of his hold and walked swiftly across the restaurant and out the door.

The afternoon session did not go smoothly. Patsy was distracted and tense and ended up claiming she was not feeling well. They canceled the session until the following day.

She went home, searched the apartment for one of the sportswear circulars; and finally found the last one buried under a stack of magazine pictures in her desk drawer. She was looking through it when the phone rang. It was Michael.

"I'm going to be here until ten, at least," he told her. "I spent most of the day seeing clients and I've got to go through the papers Alice put together to see if they're okay."

"Oh," Patsy said forlornly. "That means you won't be home until eleven."

His voice sharpened. "What's the matter, Red? Are you all right?"

Patsy hesitated and then decided to tell him about Frank later. He might feel he had to come home at once, and much as she would like that, she knew she shouldn't let him. "I'm fine," she said. "Just lonely."

"Oh." His voice changed subtly. "Well, I'll try to remedy that when I get home."

"That would be nice." Her voice was very soft. "I'll see you later, darling."

"See you later."

After she had hung up, Patsy resolutely went into the kitchen and fixed herself a dinner she really didn't want. She then turned on the TV and sat through two situation comedies she didn't hear. At ten o'clock she ran a hot tub and tried to relax. After putting on a nightgown, she got into bed with a book.

It was almost eleven-thirty when she heard Michael's key in the lock. Patsy put her book on the night table and looked up as he came into her bedroom. Miraculously, all her tension disappeared at the sight of him; and her spirits soared. "Well, well, well, Mr. Melville," she said. "It's about time."

"What a day," he grunted. "I had to tell one of my clients that he was being systematically ripped off by his warehouse manager. He was not happy." He took off his suit jacket and hung it on the back of the desk chair.

"What happened?" Patsy asked curiously.

"It's a maintenance supply firm—they sell things like toilet paper, industrial cleaners, boiler additives, stuff like that to commercial buildings and industrial parks. But the manager was also quietly selling a full order of supplies to three local private schools, who didn't know he was pocketing their payments as a nice tax-free benefit to himself." He took off his tie and draped it over his jacket.

Patsy linked her arms around her updrawn knees. "And how did you find this out?"

"Easy enough. I matched up the supplies actually on hand with the supplies that were supposed to be on hand. There was a noticeable gap between the two." His shirt had followed his tie by now.

She rested her chin on her knees. "How did you discover this gap when apparently no one else had?"

"I went to the warehouse and counted," Michael said briefly, sitting on the edge of the bed and taking off his shoes.

Patsy regarded his smoothly muscled back in admiration. "You have the most suspicious mind of anyone I've ever met. And the really sad thing is, you're usually right."

"Someone has to be suspicious," he answered, his voice a little muffled. "If only to protect the generous innocents"—he straightened up and turned around—"like you."

She reached up and ran light fingers over his cheekbone. "My knight in shining armor," she said softly, and his black brows abruptly snapped together and his face hardened.

"What is this?" he asked sharply, putting his hand on her upper arm.

Patsy had seen the marks in her bath but had quite forgotten them in the bliss of his arrival. "I had a rather unpleasant encounter with Frank Carbone," she told him in a carefully neutral voice. "You know, my partner in Ebony Lad."

"Did he do this to your arm?"

She had never seen Michael look this way. "He just held my arm for a minute," she answered hastily. "It didn't even hurt. It's just that my skin bruises so easily."

His nostrils flared a bit and then he said quietly, "I think you'd better tell me what happened."

"Well, he came to the modeling session," she began, and proceeded to detail her entire encounter with Frank. When she had finished, Michael called Frank a couple of names that provoked her heartfelt agreement. "I couldn't agree more," she said primly, "although I'm too much of a lady to say so myself."

He looked at her and his face relaxed a trifle. His eyes were now pure green. "They found they couldn't scare me off, so they decided to try you."

"That's what I figured," she replied complacently, and a flicker of amusement stirred in his cold green eyes. "The thing that really concerns me, Michael," she went on earnestly, "is, how did Frank know I was shooting for Redman Fashions?" He didn't reply. "You think this crew is tied up with the sports-clothes contract, too, don't you? That's why you've been so interested in how they advertised."

"Sweetheart," he said very gently.

"You must be right," she said. "How else would Frank have known where to find me? He must be connected with the fashion deal. He must be."

"I always said there was nothing wrong with your brain."

"The shopping centers too?" she asked hollowly.

"I don't know, Red. I'm going to fly to Illinois tomorrow and look at one of these shopping centers for myself."

"Oh," she said dismally. He was going away again.

He misunderstood her expression. "Patsy, do you want me to just hand this over to Internal Revenue? I really don't think you're in any danger, but if you're afraid, I'll turn it over tomorrow."

"Why do you want to keep it on alone, Michael?" she asked slowly. "I mean, really."

He smiled a little crookedly. "Pure egotism, sweetheart. That bastard Garfield slipped out from under once before, and I guess I just don't trust any one else to get an airtight case on him this time around."

She looked at his thin, concentrated face during a brief moment's silence, and recognized the dedication there. He really was out to make the world safe for the generous innocents—the ones like his father, whom the barracudas had destroyed. "I'm going to Illinois with you," she announced firmly.

"Oh, no," he began.

"Oh, yes," she replied very firmly.

"Patsy, I have a good friend—an ex-policeman, in fact— and I'm going to get him to come and play bodyguard for you. Just in case, you understand. You'll be far safer here than you would be with me."

Hah, she thought. So he did think he might be in danger. "Whither thou goest, I will go," she quoted, and smiled. "You can't dump me, Michael, so don't even try. That's my shopping center you're talking about, remember."

He looked down into her upturned face, and his eyes began to turn from green to gold. "I don't want to dump you, Red," he said, his voice a little deeper than usual.

Patsy lay back against her pillows and sighed very sensuously. He leaned over and put his lips to her white throat. She sighed again. "Oh, Michael," she murmured, and slid caressing hands into his thick black hair.

Chapter Ten

Patsy awoke the following morning to find Michael's arm flung across her shoulders. He was lying on his stomach, still deeply asleep, and she lay still, savoring the warmth and nearness of him. The light in the room was gray and she could hear the sound of rain on the window. The arm pinning her to the bed shifted and she turned her head on the pillow. "Good morning, darling," she said softly.

"Mmm." The long lashes lifted. "That's a nice sound to wake up to." He stirred and then sat up. "What time is it?"

She lay back on her pillow and watched him. "I don't know."

He grunted, leaned across her, and turned the bedside clock toward him. It was six-forty-five. He yawned and slid back down. "This is a damned small bed," he said.

Patsy settled herself comfortably into the curve of his arm. "It's the bed of my girlhood," she informed him. "It's bigger than a twin—Mother always called it a three-quarter bed."

"Well, it sure is cozy."

"Are you complaining?"

He chuckled. "No."

"I never noticed that it was small. But then, I've never shared it before. It's plenty big enough for one."

He didn't say anything, and she sighed. She was afraid to presume too much with him, afraid to attribute more to this affair than he. But she wanted him to know, at least a little, what it meant to her. And what she had said was true: none of her boyfriends had ever shared this bed with her. She had always attributed her reluctance to the ghost of her mother, but she realized now that it had been more than that. She sighed again.

"You sound very melancholy," he murmured near her ear.

"Do I? I suppose it's the weather."

He tightened his arm around her and she smiled. "What time do we leave for Illinois?"

"Not until this afternoon. I have to go to the office this morning. Do you want to come with me?"

"Do you want me hanging around your office all morning?" she countered.

"That way I won't have to drive back into the city to pick you up."

"I might have known it was something like that," she said without rancor. "We'll compromise. You can drop me at Sally's for the morning."

"Okay," he agreed. He kissed the top of her head. "Let's get moving, then."

She didn't stir.

His hand was slowly moving up and down her arm. "I have a few clients to see this morning."

"Mmm."

He moved away from her a little and propped himself on the arm that had been holding her close. "Circe," he murmured in a deep, slow voice.

The pillow was soft under her head, the sheets warm from the heat of their bodies. Her nightgown lay in a heap beside the bed, where he had thrown it the night before. He pulled the covers down to her waist, baring her to the cool morning air.

"Michael!" she protested, half-laughing. Then his two warm hands covered her breasts, and he bent to kiss her. She quivered under his touch, warm and yielding and sweet as honey.

"Christ," he said. "Patsy."

And she reached up to pull him closer.

They started later than Michael had planned, but he didn't complain. He dropped Patsy at Sally's and said he'd be back at about two. With his sister looking, Michael didn't kiss Patsy, but waved a casual farewell to them both as he reversed out of the driveway and turned down the street.

"Brr," remarked Sally, who was wearing jeans and a knit shirt, "it's chilly this morning. Come on in."

Patsy followed her into the kitchen, picked Matthew out of his walker, and sat with the baby on her lap.

"He's a real Melville, this one," she said to Sally as

she regarded her godchild appraisingly. "He already looks smart."

Sally grinned. "We have some pictures of Michael at that age and you'd swear they were pictures of Matthew."

"I'll bet," Patsy murmured, feeling a pang of envy. How she would love to have a baby who looked like Michael. She kissed the downy head of Michael's nephew and let him play with the gold chain around her neck.

"Michael said something about you and he going to Illinois," Sally remarked from the stove, where she was putting on coffee.

"Yes. We're going to check out one of those shopping centers Fred was always buying for me." The baby lost interest in her chain and grabbed for an enticing red-gold curl. "I have a ghastly feeling Michael doesn't think it exists."

"Oh, dear," Sally said. "I hate to tell you this, Patsy, but my brother has the most depressing habit of being right."

"Ow!" Patsy said, and removed Matthew's fingers from her hair.

Sally returned to the table. "Anyway, why are you going?" she asked curiously. "I shouldn't have thought Illinois was at all your thing."

Patsy wondered briefly whether or not to tell Sally that it wasn't Illinois but Michael who was her thing, and while she hesitated, the phone rang.

Sally picked it up. "Hello," she said impersonally, then, "Oh, hi, Jane." There was a long pause. "I know. Couldn't you just murder them?" Sally's voice dripped sympathy. "Don't worry, I'll be here all morning. There's no rush." Pause. "Okay. I'll see you later."

Sally hung up and came back to Patsy. "That was Jane Nagle, a friend of mine. She's coming over this morning, but she's been detained—her son flushed something down the toilet and stopped it all up. She's waiting for the plumber."

Patsy laughed. "Oh, dear."

"Kids," Sally said feelingly.

"How old is her son?"

"Brian—the toilet stuffer—is Steven's age. She has another son who's in school and a daughter Matthew's age. She lives right here in town and the children play well together, so we get together once a week or so."

The coffee stopped perking and Sally poured two cups. Patsy put a reluctant Matthew back in his walker and stirred milk into the cup Sally put in front of her. "Where is Steven?" she asked. "The house seems awfully quiet."

"*Sesame Street*," Sally answered succinctly.

"I just adore that show," Patsy confessed. "I'll have to go watch it with him."

Sally grinned. "The last time you were here Steven informed me that Aunt Patsy really wasn't a grown-up at all. You play just like a kid, he said."

Patsy wrinkled her nose ruefully. "I'm sure he meant it as a compliment."

"It's part of your charm," Sally assured her. Then, changing the subject, "When did Michael say he'd be back?"

"Around two."

"That's okay, then. Jane should be gone by then. She has to be back before Justin gets home from school."

"Er, is there any particular reason you don't want Michael and Jane to meet?" Patsy asked.

"Yes. You see, Jane Nagle used to be Jane Anderson."

"Oh?" said Patsy blankly.

"You probably wouldn't remember, but Jane Anderson was Michael's college girlfriend. That's how I met her. She and Michael went together for the four years he was in school. Steve and I were sure they were going to get married when they graduated."

"I see," Patsy said slowly. "What happened?"

"I don't really know." Sally put her elbows on the table. "I mean, they were inseparable for four years, and then all of a sudden Jane turned around and married Larry Nagle. It really threw me. And I have a feeling it threw Michael too."

"Do you think so?" Patsy asked hollowly.

"Yes. He's never been serious about a girl since. They always seem to be just—just—"

"Diversions," Patsy said, quoting Michael.

"Yes, diversions. I'm afraid he really loved Jane and has just never gotten over her. Jane and I ran into each other at an aerobic class at the Y shortly after Steve and I moved back to Long Island, and as I said, we've gotten together regularly since. But I'd rather Michael didn't meet her again. I'm afraid it might hurt him."

"I see your point." Patsy's face was carefully expressionless. "Poor Michael," she said.

Sally sighed. "I know. As far as I can see, the world is crawling with girls just dying to marry Michael and wouldn't you know he'd fall in love with someone who wasn't."

Patsy, who numbered among the multitudes dying to marry Michael, felt suddenly unwell. The coffee tasted bitter and her stomach was churning. She looked at the clock. "I'm going to miss *Sesame Street*," she said. She reached down and scooped up Matthew once again. "You can tidy up your kitchen and I'll entertain the kids," she informed Sally, and with Matthew tucked firmly in her arm, she went off to the family room and Kermit the Frog.

She was still in the family room, helping Steven to do puzzles, when the doorbell rang. "It's Brian!" Steven shouted, and jumped to his feet. Matthew stopped banging on his walker tray, looked at his brother, and promptly began to cry. He knew he was missing the action.

"All right, sweetie," Patsy said. "We'll go too." And with Matthew's soft warmth balanced on her hip, Patsy went out to meet the girl Michael loved.

Jane Nagle was small and slim, with long black hair and dark-blue eyes. She had a baby in her arms and a toddler at her knees, and she was laughing at Sally as she recounted her troubles with the toilet. Patsy was astonished by the physical pang of jealousy and dislike that ripped through her at the sight of Jane.

"Jane, this is my good friend Patsy Clark," Sally said.

"Hi," Jane said with a friendly smile. The blue eyes widened. "She's even more beautiful in person than she is in the magazines," she said to Sally in honest surprise. Jane had, Patsy noted sourly, a charmingly husky voice.

"I know." Sally sounded rueful. "Can you imagine what my teenage years were like, with a best friend who looks like Patsy?"

"Come off it, Sally," Patsy said with a smile. "Nice to meet you, Jane. And can you imagine how *I* felt with a best friend as smart as Sally?"

Jane grinned. "What is this? A mutual-admiration society?" Both Sally and Patsy laughed.

Jane stayed for lunch and Patsy was forced to admit that she was a lovely, charming woman. Patsy would have liked her very much if it weren't for Michael. As things stood, she disliked Jane intensely and was appalled by her own antipathy. Patsy had never been jealous in her life and was utterly unprepared to deal with such a demoralizing and primitive emotion.

Jane began to leave at one-thirty, with Sally making every effort to assist her on her way. But Megan, Jane's daughter, needed a new diaper and Brian had to go to the bathroom, so it was one-fifty by the time Jane had everyone dressed and organized. The whole crowd was in the kitchen making their farewells when the back door opened and Michael walked in.

"Michael!" Sally said instantly. "How nice that you came in time to see Jane. She's just leaving."

"Jane." Michael looked startled at first and then, as his eyes rested on the small slender figure of his former love, definitely pleased. "Jane," he repeated, and smiled. "How are you? Don't tell me these two Indians are yours?"

A very faint flush rose under Jane's fair skin. "Yes," she replied, "they are. That's Brian and this"—she shifted the baby slightly in her arms—"is Megan."

"They're beautiful," Michael said with every appearance of sincerity.

"Thank you." There was a stiffness to Jane's voice Patsy had not heard earlier. "You're looking well, Michael," she added with a visible trace of effort. The dark-blue eyes scanned his face. "You look older."

Michael grinned. "Thank's a lot, Jane. I won't return the compliment."

For the first time since he had come in, Jane smiled naturally. "I didn't mean that the way it came out. I meant you look more—more—"

"Authoritative," Patsy supplied helpfully.

"Yes." Jane looked at Patsy. "That's what I meant."

"I thought so, too," Patsy said. "I expect it comes from years and years of bossing people around."

"I never boss anyone," Michael protested.

"Hah," his sister said.

He feinted a movement toward the door. "Hey, if

this is going to continue, I'm getting out of here. Three against one is no fair."

Jane laughed. "I'm the one whose leaving. I have to get home before my other son gets back from school." She turned to Sally. "Many thanks for the lunch, Sally. I'll call you. It was nice to meet you, Patsy." Lastly, she turned to Michael. "It was good seeing you again, Michael."

Michael's face was oddly grave as he looked at her. "Good to see you too, Jane." His voice was soft. "Take care of yourself."

"Yes." She smiled brilliantly. "I will. Come on, Brian," and putting a hand on her son's shoulder, she steered him to the kitchen door.

"I'll help with the carseats," Sally offered, opening the door and following Jane out, leaving Michael and Patsy alone in the kitchen.

Patsy didn't say anything, nor did Michael, for a long moment. Then he looked at her and smiled. "Are you ready to go?"

"Pretty much. Do you want a bite of lunch? We have time."

"That's not a bad idea. God knows what rot we'll get on the plane."

"Poor baby." It was Sally coming back into the kitchen. "How about ham and cheese on rye?"

"Sounds great." Michael took off his suit jacket and hung it over the back of a kitchen chair and then sat down. He picked up Steven and sat him on his knee and said to his sister, "I didn't know you still saw Jane."

"We ran into each other a while back at the Y."

Michael began to tickle Steven. "She looks terrific," he said over the little boy's giggles. "I can't believe she has three kids."

"Um." Sally put a sandwich and a beer in front of him. "All right, Steven. Let Uncle Michael eat his lunch now."

Steven reluctantly got off Michael's lap. "Can I have a drink?" he asked in his best poor-little-waif voice.

"Sit down, Sally," Patsy said. "I'll get him something." She went to the refrigerator, trailed by the little boy.

"What are you and Patsy up to anyway?" Sally asked her brother curiously. "And what's the matter with your car that Patsy had to drive out to be your chauffeur?"

Patsy slowly poured Steven a glass of apple juice. So that's what he'd told his sister. Evidently he didn't want Sally to know he was staying with her. It was a good thing she had kept her mouth shut earlier.

"We're going to check on that Illinois shopping center of Patsy's." Michael took a long pull of beer. "Fred put quite a lot of her money into buying shares."

"Oh God, Patsy," Sally said, turning in her chair to face her. "I hope this doesn't turn out to be as bad as it sounds."

Patsy put the juice in the refrigerator and came back to the table. "Well"—she forced a smile—"we'll soon know, won't we?"

"Yep," Michael said cheerfully. He drained the last of the beer and stood up. "Time to go."

"When will you be back?" Sally asked as she accompanied them to Patsy's car.

"Possibly tomorrow—maybe the day after. It depends on what we find. We'll leave the car parked at the airport."

Patsy rolled down her window. "I don't think there's a damn thing wrong with his car," she remarked to Sally. "He just doesn't want to leave it in the long-term parking in case it gets stolen."

"It needs a new alternator," Michael said calmly. " 'Bye, Sally. I'll call you and let you know how things went."

Patsy smiled. "See you, Sal."

"I hope everything turns out okay," Sally said fervently.

"So do I." But, unlike Sally, Patsy wasn't thinking of any of her shopping centers."

Chapter Eleven

They flew into St. Louis, rented a car at the airport, crossed the Mississippi into Illinois, and headed north on Route 55.

"The shopping center is supposed to be between Alton and Springfield." Michael told her as they drove through the industrial areas of East St. Louis.

"Where would you put a shopping center here?" Patsy asked doubtfully, looking out her window at the steel mill belching smoke against the gray sky.

"It's not *here*," Michael said patiently. "It's out in the country, supposedly accessible to both farmers and city workers."

"Oh," Patsy replied even more doubtfully.

They drove through Alton, another busy manufacturing city, and then gradually the scenery changed and farms started to appear. A sign on the highway indicated that food and lodging could be found at the next exit, and Michael looked at Patsy.

"It's dinnertime," he said. "Do you want to find a motel and stop for the night or do you want to go on?"

"A motel," Patsy answered promptly. She sighed. "Do you know, Michael, I'm coming to the conclusion that I'd rather remain in ignorance about this shopping center?"

"It's too late for that now," he replied, and put the blinker signal on for the next exit. It was a gray, dark day and cars were switching on their headlights as they turned off the highway.

MOTEL, announced a neon sign on the right about a mile down the road, and a *No Vacancy* sign was underneath. Michael pulled into the drive and circled around to the office. "Wait here," he said to Patsy, got out of the car, and disappeared inside. He was back in five minutes. "Number eight," he said, driving to the back of the building.

Patsy slowly got out of the car and waited while Michael got their suitcase from the trunk. She followed him to the porch and walked through the door he was holding for her. Inside was a typical motel room, with a double bed, cheap fruitwood furniture, and tweedie commercial carpeting. The drapes were drawn, and the room was dark and chilly and smelled slightly stale.

Michael put the suitcase down and switched on the lights. "Not exactly the Taj Mahal," he said cheerfully.

"No," Patsy said. She put her purse on the dresser and stood there, gazing at it intently.

"What's wrong, Red?" Michael asked from somewhere behind her.

"Oh . . ." She shrugged her shoulders. "I don't know.

"Sorry you came?"

"No, it's not that."

"Well, then," he sounded very patient, "what is it?"

She stood where she was, her bent head affording him an excellent view of her slim back and fall of silky hair. "Do you know that scene in *A Farewell to Arms*, where Frederic and Catherine go to a hotel before he has to leave for the front?" she asked. "It's a terrible hotel, with red plush and mirrors, and Catherine says she feels like a whore. Well"— Patsy's gaze never left the expensive tan leather purse that looked so out of place on the cheap dresser top—"now I understand how she felt."

There was silence behind her, and when he spoke again, his voice was almost at her ear. "Is that the book you've been reading lately? Do I remind you of Frederic Henry?"

She shook her head and the red curls bounced against her white neck. "No. You don't remind me of anyone at all."

"Sweetheart." He put his hand on her shoulder and turned her to face him.

Her brown eyes were wide with unhappiness. "I'm sorry," she said. "It's stupid of me to play the ingenue like this. I'm hardly an innocent virgin, after all."

His arms went around her, pulling her close. "Not a virgin, perhaps, but most certainly an innocent," he murmured, his lips in her hair.

She closed her eyes and rested against him. How stupid she had been before this, she thought. How could she have mistaken the shallow emotion she had felt for love.

"Do you want to go on, after all?" he asked. "Or I could get another room for you, if you like." He sounded as if it wouldn't matter to him one way or another what she decided to do, but Patsy was too close for him to successfully disguise his feelings. He was tense with forced control. Only Michael, she thought, would understand how she felt. And only Michael wouldn't try to argue her into a more receptive frame of mind.

She raised her eyes to his. "No," she said. "I'd rather stay here with you." There was a line between his black brows as he looked intently into her eyes. She smiled. "I feel much better, Michael, really. I don't feel like a . . ." She didn't get the word out because he stopped her mouth with a long, hard kiss.

Michael's kisses were like nothing Patsy had ever known before. No one but he had ever gotten beyond the sweet serenity that was the hallmark of Patsy's personality, no one had ever touched the well of passion that lay hidden deep in the core of her. But with Michael she lost all sense of separateness; what he wanted, she wanted, and her body yielded sweetly before the pressure of his. Her eyes were closed, and when she felt the edge of the bed behind her knees, she went down willingly, drowning in passion, adrift in a land she had never found except with him.

It took a long time to recover herself again. He was lying quietly, his arms around her, his head on

her breast, and she ran gentle, caressing fingers
through his hair. A poem from one of her favorite
anthologies came slipping, unbidden, into her
mind:

Put your head, darling, darling, darling
    Your darling black head my heart above;
Oh, mouth of honey with the thyme for fragrance,
    Who with heart in breast could deny you love?

Who with heart in breast could deny you love? Certainly not me, thought Patsy, her eyes on the thick
black hair sliding so easily through her fingers. Not
ever me.

His head stirred a little. "If we're going to eat,
we'd better get going," he murmured.

Her fingers kept moving through his hair. "I
suppose," she agreed softly.

She felt the sweep of long lashes as his eyes
closed. "That feels nice." He sounded sleepy.

"There's no need to rush," she murmured.

"No."

Her hand continued its mesmerizing stroking,
and his breathing slowed. In another minute, she
knew he was asleep. She lay quietly, with the weight
of his head on her breast, and the lines of the poem
going around and around in her brain.

In the end she drifted off to sleep too and didn't
awaken until the following morning. When first she
opened her eyes, she was disoriented, not remem-
bering where she was. Then she turned her head to
look at the man beside her. He was awake, lying

propped on his elbows, watching her. She smiled, slowly and sleepily. Her glorious hair was tumbled on the pillow, her throat and shoulders bare above the drab green cover.

"Good morning," she said, her voice still husky with sleep.

"Good morning." He didn't smile back. "It's raining."

"Darn." Patsy pulled the covers over her shoulder and curled up comfortably. "What time is it?"

"Seven."

"Early," she said, snuggling her head into her pillow.

He buried his elbows in his own pillow and rested his chin on his linked hands. "First," he said, "we'll have breakfast. I'm starving. Then we'll track down this shopping center. Then I want to check out some area stores to see if your line of sportswear is on the racks."

Patsy sighed. "Simon Legree. All right. As a matter of fact, I'm starving too. And I want my shower. Do you want to shave first?"

"No. You go ahead." He sounded preoccupied and withdrawn, and he didn't even look as she got out of bed and fished in the suitcase for her wrap.

Patsy put the robe on, collected her shampoo, and hesitated, looking at his shadowed, unrevealing face. Then she walked to the bed and, bending, kissed the hard line of his cheekbone. "I adore you," she murmured and went into the bathroom. After she had gone, Michael slowly cradled his brow in his laced hands and closed his eyes.

They had breakfast at a diner a little way down the road, and since they were both hugely hungry and the service was extremely slow, it was nine o'clock before they were on the road again.

And it was an hour later, as they were driving along a road, looking at acres and acres of empty land, that Michael said, "This is where the shopping center is supposed to be."

Patsy's heart sank. Until this minute, she realized, she hadn't really let herself believe that this was going to happen. "Are you . . ." Her voice came out as a hoarse croak, and she cleared her throat and tried again. "Are you sure?"

"It's the route number specified and approximately the area. We may be a mile or so off, but there isn't a shopping center in sight, Red."

"No. There isn't."

Michael had slowed the car to fifteen miles an hour, and Patsy peered out her rain-streaked side window. "What's that over there?" she asked suddenly.

Michael pulled off the road and stopped the car. "Where?"

"Over there. See. It looks like some kind of building has been started."

"Come on, let's look."

The rain was coming down hard and a wind was blowing over the fields, but Patsy didn't complain as she trudged after Michael through the wet grass. They reached the construction Patsy had pointed out and stopped. "I'm afraid that's your shopping center, sweetheart," Michael said gently.

They were looking at the foundation of a large building. The hole had been excavated and the concrete poured and that was all. The work had evidently been done a while ago, for weeds had grown over the concrete, in some places completely obscuring it from sight.

Patsy shivered.

"Cold?" he asked, and reached out to pull her close.

Patsy pressed against him, absorbing warmth from his body. She looked up, her face wet with rain. "Oh, Michael," she said desolately.

His arm tightened. "I'm going to get them, sweetheart. We'll see if we can get some of your money back."

"It isn't the money, really." She stared at the bleak, rain-sodden foundation. "It's the rottenness of it all. That Fred could do this to me."

"Dante put the traitors in the bottom circle of hell," he said.

She shivered again. He had spoken very quietly but something in his voice frightened her. She was suddenly glad she was the victim of this particular scam and not the perpetrator.

"Come on, Red," he said, and his voice sounded more normal. "Let's get out of here. You're freezing."

They drove into the nearest town and dried off in a coffee shop. Then they went department-store-browsing. They ended the day by driving back into

Alton and browsing there as well. In no store did they find a trace of Patsy Clark sportswear.

"That's it, then," Patsy said glumly as they returned to the car after their last excursion. "The sportswear is a bust, too."

He looked at his watch. "Do you want to get the eight-o'clock plane?"

"Yes."

He smiled a little at her tone and started up the car. "Okay. Let's head for the airport. There has to be a restaurant somewhere nearby where we can eat and get a drink."

Patsy leaned her head against the car seat. "Several drinks, I think," she murmured, and he grunted in assent.

They stopped at a steak place not far from the airport, and Patsy went into the bathroom, where she washed her hands and face, put on new blush and lipstick, and tied her hair back with a scarf. Her candy-striped blouse was undoubtedly a mass of wrinkles, but the cotton knit sweater she wore hid most of it. Her green blazer and pink sailcloth pants, however, had never recovered from their earlier soaking. Oh, well, Patsy thought resignedly, glamour isn't everything, I suppose, and went out to rejoin Michael.

Over their first cocktail she brought up the subject that had been puzzling her all day. "I understand about the shopping center, Michael. Fred simply passed my money along to his friends in the guise of buying me shares. What I don't understand is the sportswear. I got paid for endorsing that sportswear. I got paid quite a lot—almost a million and a half last year, if I remember correctly."

He took a long sip of Scotch. "You remember correctly."

"But why pay me for something that doesn't exist?" She stared at him in utter bewilderment. "It doesn't make sense to give me money and then to rob me of it. I just can't figure it out."

He regarded her over the rim of his glass. "I think they were using you to launder illegal money, Red."

Her brow furrowed. "What do you mean?"

"Let's say that you have a lucrative but illegal enterprise going—you're selling drugs, for instance. You're making a lot of money and you want to be able to spend it. You want nice cars, a big house, furs for your wife, et cetera. But you can't account for the money legally."

"So?" Patsy asked. "The Cadillac salesman doesn't care where your money came from, Michael."

He put his glass down. "No. But the IRS does." Patsy's eyes widened. He smiled a little at her expression. "If someone who has no known source of income suddenly starts spending big bucks on consumer items, the IRS will want to know where that money came from."

"The light begins to dawn," Patsy said softly.

"Garfield is connected with drug traffic—there isn't much doubt of that. I think they set you up with that phony sportswear contract as a way of getting the drug money legally into Garfield's pocket. They created this fashion company and produced a limited line of clothes which they made advertising circulars for. You did the advertising and Fred showed the circulars to the IRS. He also showed the IRS that you cleared a profit of one and a half million on the clothes. The books are all in order. The paperwork for Redman Fashions and for the shopping center is brilliant. There are full records on everything. No one would be likely to suspect anything—unless, of course, one actually went out to look for the imaginary products."

"As we just did."

"As we just did," he agreed.

"So this Garfield was on both ends of the money, then," Patsy said thoughtfully.

"That's right. He funneled the money in through the fashion deal, then—as owner of the Crossmal Shopping Center—he collected it at the other end. Only now the money was legal and accounted for." Michael signaled the waiter and ordered another round of drinks. "I wonder who else Fred was working for?" he asked after the waiter had gone.

"Do you think he was doing the same thing to his other clients?"

"I'd bet on it."

Patsy was frowning at her empty Scotch sour. "But, Michael, if it's as you just said, then I wasn't robbed at all. I mean, the money wasn't really mine to begin with."

"Did you get paid for the hours you put in to do the fashion advertising?"

"No. That was included in the deal."

"You're out a chunk of your time, then—and very expensive time it is, too, sweetheart. Also you haven't pursued other contracts because you thought you were making good money from this one. And," he concluded gently, "we haven't even mentioned Fred's little account in the Cayman Islands."

"Oh, that."

"Yes, that. Fred didn't have a clever scam to make that money legal, so he just put it away where the IRS wouldn't find it. On the other hand, it's still there, and I have the bankbook. We should be able to recover that for you anyway, Patsy."

"I'll probably have to pay taxes on it," Patsy said resignedly, and he grinned.

"You will, sweetheart. You most certainly will."

They returned the car to the airport rental agency and boarded the plane to New York. Michael was preoccupied for most of the trip, frowning slightly and making notes in a small black leather book. Patsy pulled a novel out of her purse and read. When the Fasten Your Seatbelt sign came on, she put her book away and turned to look at Michael's face, her eyes lingering lovingly on his brow line and cheekbone. He glanced at her, and she smiled.

His preoccupied look lifted. "Sorry to be such lousy company," he murmured.

"I don't mind." Her smile was ineffably lovely. "You don't have to entertain me, Michael."

His eyes glinted and slowly began to change from

green to gold. Patsy gazed at him in fascination. "I can't believe we only met again two weeks ago," she said softly.

"Mmm." He put his notebook away and took her wrist in his hand. "An awful lot has happened in two weeks." He moved his thumb caressingly along her palm.

"Michael . . ." She made no attempt to hide what she was feeling. She had never had any practice in the art of deception. Besides, he must feel the pulse hammering in her wrist.

"We'll be home soon," he said in a low voice.

Wordlessly, she nodded.

Chapter Twelve

'Who with heart in breast could deny you love?" was the refrain that went through Patsy's brain the following morning when she awoke in his arms. Then he began to kiss her throat, her shoulders, and all thought was suspended for quite some time.

The refrain came back, however, while she made him breakfast and kissed him good-bye as he went off to the office. It was in her mind as she straightened the bedroom and cleared away the breakfast dishes. Just to wash his coffeecup made her so damn happy. She shook her head ruefully at her own emotion, but her heart was full of tenderness all the same.

The rain that had soaked the area the previous night had lifted, and the sun looked as if it might be going to burn through the haze. Deciding to go for a run in the park, Patsy went into her bedroom to put on running clothes. She looked mournfully at her name, emblazoned so confidently on the deep-purple sweatshirt, then tied a scarf around her forehead to keep the hair off her face. She hummed all the way down in the elevator. Michael might not love her as she did him, but he wanted her. Of that she was quite certain. It was something to build on, she thought.

"Good morning, Miss Clark."

It was Tom, the day doorman, and she smiled at him, gave him a sunny greeting, and went out onto Central Park West. She was standing at the corner, waiting for the light, when a gray car with tinted windows pulled up in front of her and stopped. At the same moment a voice said in her ear, "All right, baby, don't make a sound and get into the car." There was the distinctly unpleasant feeling of something poking into her back.

The car door opened and the man behind her gave a shove. Before Patsy quite understood what was happening, she found herself in the back seat. The door slammed and the car took off at high speed.

"How are you, beautiful?" asked a voice beside her, and she turned, only to look into the darkly handsome face of Frank Carbone.

Her hands went icy cold "Fr-Frank," she said breathlessly. "What's this all about?"

"It's about you and Michael Melville, Miss Clark," a voice from the front seat said, and Patsy looked up at the heavy-jowled face of Jack Garfield. The cold spread from her hands to her heart.

For a long minute there was silence in the car. The man from the sidewalk had gotten into the back seat after her, and Patsy was securely jammed between his burly body and Frank. She wasn't going to be able to get out.

The car stopped for a light and Patsy looked out the window and saw a policeman. Without pausing to reflect on the wisdom of her action, she filled her lungs with air and opened her mouth to scream.

A brutal hand clamped down over her mouth. Patsy struggled and finally succeeded in biting the palm that was pressing her lips against her teeth so mercilessly. She must have hurt him, for she heard him swear, and then he grabbed her head and rammed it hard into his chest. The car began to move forward again.

"Let's get the hell out of the city," Frank said breathlessly. The pressure of his hand on the back of Patsy's head was extremely painful. Her nose and mouth were crushed against him and his jacket button was gouging her cheek. She struggled more, but he only held her tighter. She was having a hard time breathing. Finally, she went limp.

"That's better," Frank said. The pressure on the back of her head eased very slightly, making it easier for her to breathe.

"Keep her like that." It was Jack Garfield's voice from the front seat. "We don't want to have to knock her out. We need her to get Melville for us."

"Sure," Frank said. "It's a pleasure. Just be quiet, beautiful," he said to Patsy, "and you won't get hurt."

Patsy was still as stone. What did they mean, they needed her to get Michael for them? Dear God, dear God, dear God. What were they going to do?

Frank's hand, which had been gripping her shoulder, moved down her back. "I've thought about having you like this," he said. "Thought about it a lot." His hand moved again and fondled her breast. Patsy went rigid.

"Not now, Frank," ordered the voice from the front seat.

There was a pause, then the hand gave her breast a cruel squeeze and withdrew. "All right." The grip on her head tightened, and the button ground into her cheek. "I'll wait."

Patsy had not thought it possible to be this frightened. Her face pressed painfully against Frank's chest, she tried frantically to think of a way out of this.

The ride seemed interminable. She decided that the best time to make a move was when they were taking her out of the car. She'd try to scream then, she thought. Even if they shot her, she had to try something. She couldn't just let Michael walk into the middle of a trap.

They went through a toll, but Garfield raised the tinted glass partition that separated the front and back seats, and Patsy remained undiscovered. Finally, after what seemed to her an eternity, the car came to a halt and the engine was switched off.

"All right," Garfield said, "Frank and I will take her into the house. Herbie, drive the car down the street and wait there. We don't want Melville to suspect anything. Joe, you come with us."

The door next to Frank opened. "All right, beautiful," Frank said, "no tricks now." His hold on her head relaxed, and Patsy cautiously lifted her face, blinking in the sunshine. Her neck ached. She looked around and realized, with deep surprise, that they were at Michael's house. She wet her lips and tried to keep her face expressionless. There was no one in sight, but surely someone was home, someone would hear her.

The man behind her wrenched her arm so that it was almost all the way up her back. The pain was excruciating. "All right now, baby," his voice said in her ear. "We're going to walk into the house. Quietly, or I'll break your arm for you."

Frank got out of the car and Patsy followed, doubled over with agony in her arm. The two men hovered over her solicitously, or so it would appear to any disinterested observer. Patsy felt sweat break out all over her body. She was incapable of uttering a sound.

They reached the house, and as the door closed behind them, the grip on Patsy's arm loosened and she was free. She stood in the living room, trembling violently and feeling ill as Frank locked the door and drew the curtains across the picture window. Then he turned to her.

"All right, beautiful," he said pleasantly, "now you're going to put in a call to the boyfriend."

Patsy swallowed and didn't say anything. The man called Joe took out his gun and aimed it at her stomach.

Jack Garfield took over. "You call him and tell him to come here. And get him here without making him suspect anything is wrong. Be very careful." He nodded to the gunman. "Joe here is very nervous."

Patsy wet her lips. "It's crazy. I mean, there isn't any reason for me to be here."

"Tell him you wanted to finish cleaning up the mess," Frank suggested.

"Were you the ones who wrecked the house?" she asked, playing for time.

"We were hoping very much that you and Melville would get the message from that little decorating job," Garfield said regretfully. "But when you flew out to St. Louis, I knew you hadn't."

Patsy felt as if she had just been kicked in the stomach. She clenched her fists until she felt the nails score into her palms. "And if I say I won't call Michael?"

"Then," Garfield said simply, "I would have to make you. Or Frank would."

Patsy swallowed. "All right. I'll call him."

"Very sensible. Now what are you going to tell him?"

"He's using my car. I'll tell him that I wanted the two cars in New York and came out here to drive his back, but it won't start. I'll tell him I'm afraid to stay here alone and ask him to come and get me."

"Melville did take her car this morning, Jack," Frank said.

"Yeah. You tell him that. And remember, no tricks."

"Okay."

He gestured her over to the phone and stood next to her. Patsy picked up the receiver, but her

hand was shaking too much for her to dial. Garfield
got the number for her.

"Lawson and Melville," said a woman's impersonal voice.

"Is Mr. Melville there please?" Patsy asked. "This
is Patricia Clark calling."

"One moment, please, Miss Clark."

There were some beeping sounds and then
Michael's voice came over the wire. "What's up,
Red?"

"Oh, Mike," Patsy said hurriedly, "I'm so glad
you're in. I'm afraid I've gotten myself into a bit of a
jam."

There was a brief pause. "What's happened? Are
you all right?"

"Oh, yes, I'm fine, Mike. But I'm here at your
house and I'm stuck. I got a friend to drive me out
so I could get your car, and then I decided to do
some tidying up while I was here. But when I went
out to start the car to go back to New York, it
wouldn't start."

"Where's your friend?"

"She left. She just dropped me off—she's going
out to Fire Island. Do you think you could come
over and pick me up, Mike? I'm getting nervous
here by myself. Those awful thugs might come
back."

"I'm with a client right now, Pat. Can you wait
there for half an hour or so?"

"Of course."

"I'll be there as soon as I can, sweetheart. Lock
the door and don't let anyone in."

"Okay, Mike. I'll be waiting." She hung up and looked at Jack Garfield.

He nodded. "Very good." He gestured her to the sofa. "Sit down." Slowly Patsy crossed the floor and sat, her sneakered feet pressed together on the floor, her hands clasped tensely in her lap. The man with the gun sat in a chair across from her, and Frank and Garfield went to the curtained window. The room was very quiet. Patsy prayed.

It was forty-five minutes later when she heard the sound of a car pulling into the driveway. A door slammed, and from the window Frank said, "It's him."

Patsy's knuckles went white with pressure as she watched the door with huge, frightened eyes. There was the sound of a key in the lock, and then the knob turned, the door opened, and Michael was there.

Frank, who had been standing behind the door, slammed it shut. Joe stepped out from the dining area, gun in hand, and Garfield said, "Melville. At last."

Michael's eyes went to Patsy, sitting frozen and terrified on the sofa. "I'm so sorry, Michael," she said miserably.

He was impeccably dressed in a business suit, white shirt, and dark striped tie. His eyes went from her to the three men who now circled him, and for a brief, startling second his face was totally out of character with his civilized garb. "Who did that to your face?" he asked.

Patsy put her hand up to her sore cheek. "Oh," she said, "that was Frank's button."

"The bruise on her cheek is only a sample of what's going to happen, Melville," Frank threatened.

"I know about the shopping center," Michael said. His face now looked cold and composed. "I know about the fashion contract."

Garfield swore.

"And," Michael continued evenly, "I have lodged all of this information with my lawyer, with instructions that it be delivered to the IRS."

"I don't believe you," Garfield said. "You didn't have time. You only got back from St. Louis last night."

Michael stood very still. "I did it this morning."

Frank let loose with a long string of obscenities. Michael ignored him and continued to look at Garfield with narrowed eyes. "If anything should happen to either Patricia Clark or myself," he continued calmly, "you'll be charged with murder."

There was a long silence fraught with tension. Then Garfield said, "Get the papers back from your lawyer."

"No," Michael said.

Joe's gun moved from Michael to Patsy. She sat up straight, her back not touching the sofa, and said bravely, "Don't be an ass. If you shoot me, he'll never get you those papers." She looked from Joe to Michael and found a faint, approving smile in his eyes. Unaccountably, she felt much better.

Garfield gestured and the gun swung back to

Michael. "We're not going to shoot you, Miss Clark. Frank has a very different idea about what to do with you. Would you like to watch, Melville?"

Michael stared at Garfield, and Patsy found herself recoiling from what she read in Michael's eyes. "I'll call him," he said flatly. He looked at Frank, and Patsy began to shiver convulsively. Michael walked over to the telephone and picked up the receiver.

"Stan?" he said when he had gotten through. "You know that package I had delivered to you this morning? Well, I need it. Yes, right now. Can you send someone to my house with it? No, it can't wait. Yes, I'm at home now. All right. I'll be waiting. Yes. Thanks." He rang off and looked at Garfield. "He's sending someone over with it."

Patsy looked at Michael's bleak face and swallowed hard. They're going to kill us, she thought incredulously. They'll have to. Oh, my *God.*

"On the sofa, Melville," Garfield instructed. "We'll wait."

Michael crossed the room and sat next to Patsy. Wordlessly he put out an arm and pulled her close. Patsy pressed against him, taking comfort from his nearness, his warmth, his calm. His calm. With a start she realized that the heartbeat she could feel so reassuringly against her shoulder was steady and unhurried. The breath that stirred the fine hair above her ear was even and slow. He wasn't afraid, she thought in astonishment. He wasn't afraid at all.

They sat like that, in perfect silence, for what

seemed like an eternity. In reality, it was about five minutes. Then there was the sound of a loud-speaker outside the house.

"This is the police. Come out with your hands up."

Frank swore and looked at Michael. So did the other two.

"The police have all the documents, Garfield," Michael said calmly and coldly. "And they have the house surrounded." He had moved so that Patsy was now behind him on the sofa. "Give up."

"The house is surrounded," came the loud-speaker in eerie echo of Michael's words. "Surrender with your hands up."

Frank ran into the kitchen and looked out the window. "Jesus, they're all over the place."

"You bastard." Garfield swore. "You goddamn bastard!" His voice vibrated with hate, and Michael stood up and moved away from Patsy. Shaking with fury, Garfield reached out and grabbed the gun from Joe. "I'm gonna fix you, I'm gonna fix you good," he muttered, and raised the muzzle.

"Michael!" Patsy screamed in pure terror, and a fraction of a second later, Michael dived to his left as the gun went off. Then the front door was smashed in, and the room was full of police. Patsy ran to Michael, who was lying on the ground, his blue pin-striped trouser leg stained with a spreading tide of red.

Chapter Thirteen

When Michael saw her kneeling beside him, he tried to sit up.

"Stay right where you are," she said sharply. "Your leg is bleeding badly. He might have hit an artery." A policeman appeared at her shoulder and she asked, "Do you have a first-aid kit?" The man ran for the door, and Patsy said to Michael, "Don't move, darling," and began searching in her purse for her manicure scissors.

"Sorry I let you in for such a lousy time, Red," he said breathlessly as she cut his trouser leg to get at the wound in his thigh. There was a great deal of blood.

"I'd better put on a tourniquet," said the policeman returning with the first-aid kit, and Patsy knelt next to Michael's shoulder as the officer competently went to work. Behind them Garfield and friends were being handcuffed and removed to waiting patrol cars.

"There was another man," Patsy said suddenly. "A man in a gray car."

"Don't worry, ma'am. We got him." Another officer came to stand over them. "An ambulance is on the way," he said.

Michael lifted heavy eyelids and looked up. "Thanks. You were right on schedule."

"He shot you after we arrived."

"Yes." A ghost of a smile flickered across Michael's white face. "Vengeance, I'm afraid. I hadn't thought of that." His eyes were black with pain as they moved from the policeman to Patsy. "Are you okay?" he asked.

"I'm fine, darling." She grasped his hand and kissed the long, slender fingers. "And you will be, too. Just hold on a little longer—the ambulance will be here soon."

He nodded. "Will you call Steve, Patsy? Tell him what happened?"

Of course. Steve, the orthopedic surgeon. "I'll call him right now. Perhaps he can meet us at the hospital." Patsy leaned down and touched her lips lightly to his temple, as if she were afraid a harder touch would hurt him, then she stood and went to the telephone.

Fortunately Steve was just out of surgery and she was able to get him after a five-minute wait. While she was on the phone, the ambulance arrived, and after she had hung up, she went over to where they were putting Michael on a stretcher. He was still conscious but very pale.

"Can't you give him something for the pain?" she asked a medic urgently.

"We'll be at the hospital in five minutes, miss," he

answered reassuringly. "The doctors there will probably give him something. Are you coming in the ambulance?"

"Yes, I am." Patsy ran to get her purse and then followed the stretcher out to the waiting ambulance.

They were racing through the streets, siren blaring, when Michael opened his eyes and looked at her. "You warned me," he said. "Smart girl."

"I didn't know if you would understand me." She thought talking might help to take his mind off the pain and so she continued. "And when you turned up alone, I was afraid you hadn't."

"It took me a while to convince the police of the urgency of the situation. Then I had to call Stan Kavan and explain what I would be doing." His voice was low but clear.

"You mean you hadn't left the papers with him?"

A faint smile flickered in his clouded eyes. "No. The phone call was a signal that it was okay for the police to move in."

She smiled back.

"Sorry to put you through such a bad time." He put a hand up to her face. "The bastard," he said.

"I got off lighter than you. I was more scared than hurt."

"I'm sorry," he repeated.

"Darling, it was my mess to begin with. I'm the one who should be apologizing."

"No." His brow was furrowed with pain. "It was my goddamn arrogance. I should have turned this whole mess over to the IRS last week. It's only luck that you weren't badly hurt." His shadowed eyes searched her face. "That swine Frank didn't try anything with you, did he?"

"No." She shook her head. "Except for pushing my face into his chest to keep me quiet, he didn't touch me."

Michael's eyes closed. "Thank God."

Patsy spoke to the medic riding with them. "When are we going to get to the hospital?"

"We're coming in now, miss," he told her, and she looked out the window and saw the sign EMERGENCY and an arrow. In thirty seconds they were at the emergency-room door, and the medics were lifting Michael out.

They wouldn't let her go past the reception area, and she got stuck answering a lot of questions for the woman at the admissions desk. They brought her Michael's wallet and she got out his Blue Cross card. Then she sat on a curved plastic seat and stared at the poster on the opposite wall describing the Heimlich maneuver.

She was still there thirty minutes later when Steve arrived. She heard someone say her name, and looked up to see him striding toward her.

"Steve! Thank God you're here. I don't know what they're doing to Michael."

"They're prepping him for surgery. I'm going to take the bullet out. Jesus God, Patsy, what happened?" He sat next to her.

She was very pale, her eyes huge and dark and frightened, but she spoke calmly. She was not, he was extremely gratified to see, going to have hysterics. "It was my taxes, Steve. Michael discovered Fred was using me to launder illegal drug money. Fred's boss found out and came after Michael."

"Jesus God," Steve repeated.

Patsy drew a deep, uneven breath. "Yes. Is he going to be all right?"

"His life's not in danger, but it's a damn good thing someone got a tourniquet on him."

"And his leg?"

"I don't know. I'll have to see. Will you call Sally? She doesn't know what's happened yet."

"Of course I will."

"Good girl."

He turned to leave, and Patsy put out a hand to detain him. "Steve, you'll come and tell me when you've finished?"

His long-fingered, sensitive, surgeon's hand covered hers for a brief moment. "I'll come as soon as I can."

"Thanks." She managed a smile. "I'll call Sally now."

His hand tightened over hers for a second, and then he was gone.

"Patsy!"

She turned from her mesmerized perusal of the Heimlich maneuver to see Sally coming across the waiting room toward her. The other people in the room watched with interest as the gorgeous red-head in the jogging suit rose and embraced the worried-looking, dark-haired woman who had just entered. Then the two of them sat down side by side and began to talk in low-pitched, urgent voices.

"Is he still in the operating room?" Sally asked.

"He must be. Steve said he'd come down as soon as he could."

"Steve's a very good surgeon," Sally said. "He won't let anything happen to Michael."

There was a short silence, then Patsy asked, "Who has the kids?"

"Jane Nagle came over and got them. She'll keep them until we get back."

"Oh. That was nice of her."

"Yes. She was almost as upset about Michael as I was, I think."

Silence fell between them again and lasted until Steve appeared in the waiting room twenty minutes later. He was still in green operating-room garb and he smiled, immediately and reassuringly, as he saw his wife. "He's going to be fine, Sally. He won't be too comfortable for a while, but I don't think there's been any permanent damage done."

Patsy felt suddenly dizzy with relief. "Thank God," she breathed, and then Steve's arm was around her shoulders.

"Here," he said imperatively, "sit down and put your head between your knees. I don't want you fainting on me now." He guided Patsy to a chair and said over his shoulder to his wife, "Ask the nurse at the desk inside for smelling salts."

Patsy sat and obediently hung her head, and in a minute Steve held something to her nostrils that made her eyes water. "Whew!" she said.

"Better?"

"Yes." Her head felt quite clear now and cautiously she raised it. Steve and Sally were both looking at her in concern. "I'm so sorry," she said contritely. "That was stupid of me."

"Not at all," Steve said. "You've had one hell of a day. You're entitled." He had his hand on her wrist, feeling her pulse.

She smiled a little and some of the color began to return to her face. "I'm okay, really."

He released her wrist and nodded. "Just sit quietly for a few minutes, please."

"Can I see him?" Sally asked.

"He's still under the anaesthetic, Sally. They'll keep him in the recovery room for a few more hours at least." Steve looked at his watch. "Wait until tomorrow morning. He's not going to feel much like visitors before then." He looked at his wife. "You didn't have to come. Where are the kids?"

"At Jane Nagle's. And I just couldn't sit quietly at home."

He smiled. "I know. Well, how many cars do we have here now?"

"Mine is still at Michael's house," Patsy said.

"Leave it there for now. You're in no condition to drive, Patsy. Why don't you take Patsy, babe, and go collect the kids. I'll be home in another couple of hours. I have to change and see a few people—the hospital was very accommodating in letting me operate, since I'm not affiliated here. And I want to engage a private duty nurse for Mike."

"Okay." Under the interested eyes of the watching waiting room, Sally fervently kissed the tall,
lean doctor and was kissed back quite as heartily.

"He's going to be fine," Steve reassured her.

"I know." She smiled at him. "Doctor Maxwell."
Sally turned to Patsy. "Come on, Patsy. I'm going to
take you home, fill you with alcohol, and you're
going to tell me everything."

"Wait until I get there," Steve said. "This is one
story I don't want to miss."

Sally and Patsy stopped by Jane Nagle's house
and picked up the children. Jane did indeed seem
very upset; there was the unmistakable sheen of
tears in her eyes when Sally told her Michael was
going to be all right.

"What's Jane's husband like?" Patsy asked Sally as
they drove the two miles between the Nagle and
Maxwell houses.

"He's a very pleasant fellow. Works down on Wall
Street for a brokerage firm." There was silence and
then Sally added, "He's not a patch on Michael,
though. And that is not just sisterly prejudice,
either."

Patsy smiled painfully. "I'm sure it isn't."

When they reached Sally's, Patsy cleaned up in
the bathroom and then helped to feed Matthew
and Steven. She had eaten nothing herself since
breakfast, but she wasn't hungry. She did drink a
cup of hot tea and then volunteered to give Steven
his bath. She was just getting the little boy into his
pajamas when Steve came home.

They put the children to bed and then sat in the living room, with stiff drinks and a huge plate of cheese and crackers to nibble on.

"All right, Patsy," Sally said. "I've been a model of patience. Tell. What on earth happened that my brother ended up in the hospital with a bullet in his leg?"

Patsy took a drink of Scotch, ate a cheese cracker, and started her story. "We got back to New York last night," she was saying four cheese crackers later, "and Michael drove me home. It was very late so he stayed at my apartment." She pretended not to notice the look Sally and Steve exchanged. "He left for work this morning and, naturally, he took my car. Garfield and Frank saw him go."

"If they wanted Michael, and if they were watching you, why did they let him go to work?" Sally asked.

"I don't imagine they could get to him," Steve answered. "Patsy's building is like a Norman fortress, and he drove right out of the garage onto a busy New York street."

"I'm sure that was it," Patsy agreed. "And so they decided to wait for me."

She proceeded to tell them all about her kidnapping and the ride to Michael's house.

"Patsy!" Sally looked appalled. "You must have been terrified."

"Terrified isn't the half of it." Patsy's look was eloquent. "Well, once we got to the house they made me call Michael." Her lips tightened. "I didn't want to, but they were waving a very unfriendly-looking gun."

"God Almighty," Sally gasped.

"I knew I had to warn Michael. I couldn't just let him walk in blindly, but Garfield was standing right next to me and listening to every word we both said."

"You *did* warn him," Steve said suddenly. "You must have. He brought the police with him."

"What did you do?" Sally asked.

"I called him Mike. I've never once called him Mike in my entire life, but I called him Mike on the phone constantly. It was all I could think of. And, when he called me Pat back, I thought he'd understood. But then he marched in all alone, and I thought they were going to kill us both."

"Have another drink," Steve said.

"And you think I'm smart." Sally's voice rang with admiration. "How *clever* of you, Patsy. However did you think of that?"

"I read it in a mystery novel once," Patsy answered with simple truth, and took the glass Steve held out to her.

He grinned. "You're a great girl, Patsy."

She smiled back. "Thank you, Doctor. It was Michael who thought to call you, though. He was lying there, bleeding all over the floor, and he looked up and said, quite calmly, 'Call Steve and tell him what's happened.' "

"What I want to know," Steve said, "is why Michael felt he had to play detective himself. Why the hell didn't he just tell the Justice Department all he knew? Christ, he used to work there. He has friends."

"Michael had the goods on Garfield once before," Patsy explained, "and from what I gather, someone botched up the case. He wanted to make sure it didn't happen again."

"If that isn't just like him," Sally said with the faintest trace of bitterness. "My brother the crusader."

"He is, you know." Patsy spoke very softly. "He's not trying to be heroic or anything, he just can't bear the thought of people like Garfield going around destroying people like your father."

"I know." The bitterness had left Sally's voice. "It doesn't just go back to Daddy, either. Michael was always like that. Even when he was a little kid, he always stuck up for the underdog."

"I remember." Patsy's voice was softer than before.

Steve stretched. "Well, this cheese is fine as far as it goes, but what's for dinner? I'm starving, woman."

"Then just take yourself over to the telephone and call out for pizza," his wife answered sweetly.

Steve grunted. "Pizza, huh?"

"Pizza."

"Oh, all right." He got to his feet. "How do you like yours, Patsy?"

"With sausage," she answered promptly. She, too, was suddenly ravenous.

"You'll stay the night, of course," Sally said.

"I was certainly planning to."

Sally grinned. "It's a good thing I've got a spare room. Michael will be it's next occupant, I suppose. I hope he doesn't have to stay in the hospital too long."

"I hope so," Patsy echoed, and hoped also that her face was not indicative of her hurt feelings. Of course Sally would expect to take care of her brother. She herself certainly had no claim. She felt tears sting her eyes and hastily looked down to hide them. God, she never cried. She must be more tired than she thought.

Chapter Fourteen

❧

Sally and Patsy dropped the children at Jane Nagle's the following morning and proceeded across the island to the hospital. Steve had left the house earlier and called before they set off to say that Michael was doing as well as could be expected.

His leg was in some sort of cradle and there was an IV in his arm. He was unshaven and haggard yet when he saw the two of them walk into the room, he grinned. "Come to view the fallen warrior?"

"Oh, Michael!" Sally went to the bed and kissed him.

"I know," he said comfortingly. "It was stupid of me to get shot."

Sally laughed shakily. "It certainly was. But I must confess, it's impressed Steven enormously."

He laughed at that, as he was meant to, and then his eyes moved from his sister's face to Patsy's. She was dressed in the same clothes she had worn yesterday and the bruise on her cheek had turned the same interesting shade of purple as her outfit. He eyes were huge and brilliant in her pale face. The expression on his face did not alter and he said, "You even manage to look beautiful with a bruise on your cheek."

"I know," Sally said. "It's disgusting, really." She pulled a chair up to Michael's bedside. "How are you feeling, Michael?"

"Lousy," he replied frankly, his attention moving from Patsy back to his sister. "Steve assures me that he repaired all the damages, however, so I can't complain too loudly. The bullet missed the bone, thank God. A smashed-up thighbone would not have been fun." He moved his head a little on the pillow. "It was very clever of you, Sal," he added, "to marry a surgeon."

"I was thinking ahead," she replied readily.

He laughed and shifted slightly once again. Patsy looked at his hands, clenched tightly on the edge of the blanket, out of sight of Sally's eyes but not of hers.

"I'll be right back," she murmured, and slipped out of the room and down to the nurses' station. "Mr. Melville is in a considerable amount of pain," she told the nurse behind the desk crisply. "Didn't Doctor Maxwell prescribe something for him?"

"I'll look," the nurse said pleasantly, and consulted a chart. Then she looked at her watch. "He was supposed to get something two hours ago."

"And he didn't?"

"No. I'll come now and give him a shot."

"Thank you," Patsy said, and walked back down

the hall, inwardly raging. Two hours! Wait until Steve heard.

Michael was still talking to Sally when Patsy reentered the room. His eyes went immediately to her face and she smiled at him, a smile like warm sunlight in the small and sterile hospital room. "Where did you go?" Sally asked.

A nurse with a hypodermic in her hand then entered behind Patsy. "Time for a shot, Mr. Melville," she said cheerfully. "You should have rung if the pain was getting bad." Michael didn't say anything but looked once again at Patsy. "If you'll excuse us for one moment," the nurse said to Sally and pulled the curtains around Michael's bed.

"How late was that shot?" Sally demanded after the nurse had left.

"Two hours," Patsy replied.

"Why didn't you ring for the nurse?" Sally asked Michael.

He shrugged. He looked exhausted, Patsy thought. "I don't know what I'm supposed to get."

Sally went to look at the chart at the bottom of the bed. "Every four hours," she said. "If they don't give you another shot in four hours, for God's sake, ring."

"All right." His eyes were already beginning to close.

"Come on, Sally. He's going to sleep," Patsy said softly.

"All right." Sally bent to kiss her brother once again. "I'll be back tomorrow, Michael."

Patsy came up after Sally, and she too leaned

down and gently kissed the hair that slanted across his forehead. He looked at her for a brief moment. His pupils were already dilated from the drug; his eyes looked black. She wanted nothing more than to sit at his bedside all day and watch over him. But she had no claim. "Take care of yourself," she whispered, and then, with extreme reluctance, she stepped back and followed Sally out of the room.

Michael was in the hospital for almost two weeks. Patsy moved back to New York, and in between answering a lot of questions for the Justice Department, she drove out to Long Island five times to see him. But there was always someone there—Sally or a friend or, on one occasion, the same man from the Justice Department who had questioned her.

There was a barrier between them, and it wasn't just the presence of other people. Patsy didn't know what it was, but she was sensitive to the fact that Michael had retreated from her. He was perfectly pleasant, perfectly friendly, but that he had put up a barrier, she had no doubt at all.

At first Patsy tried to tell herself it was because he was ill and in pain. It would get better, she thought, once he got out of the hospital.

He left the hospital on a Monday and on Tuesday Patsy drove to Sally's to see him. He was lying on the sofa in the living room reading the newspaper when she came in. He was fully clothed and stretched out like a schoolboy. A set of crutches was propped up against the wall next to the sofa. Patsy sat on a chair and they talked under the in-and-out-again eye of Sally and in the almost continual presence of Steven. Patsy, who genuinely loved Sally and her family, wished fervently that they would all go away and give her just a half an hour alone with Michael. Then perhaps she would be able to discover what had happened between them.

She did a cover for a national magazine and shot another camera commercial. The newspapers had gotten wind of her kidnapping, and she found herself besieged by reporters. The Justice Department issued a statement on the subject and warned her to say nothing further. Michael began to walk with the help of a cane and planned to move back into his own home shortly.

During this stressful time Patsy remained her usual serene, unruffled self. She was polite with the obstreperous reporters, patient with her mother, professional with the cameramen. She was also deeply and profoundly unhappy. She had not known it was possible to be so unhappy.

He didn't love her, no longer wanted her, and that it seemed was that. There was nothing she could do. She had found the one man in the world for her, and then she had lost him. And nothing would ever be the same again. It was as simple, and as devastating, as that.

Michael called her one day to say he had ironed out her situation with the IRS and did she want to come out and discuss it with him? She agreed, and on a dismal gray and rainy day, she drove once again out to Michael Melville's house.

He answered the door dressed in chino pants and

a dark-green knit golf shirt. He was not using a cane and there was only a slight hesitation in his walk as he led her into the living room.

"The house looks considerably better than it did the last time I was here," she remarked.

"I got a cleaning service in and I had the walls all repainted."

"You also bought some new chairs."

"Sally got them for me at some sale."

"They're very nice." She sat in one of them and looked at him gravely.

He sat on the sofa and picked up a paper. "Well, let's get this straightened out, shall we?" His voice was professional, impersonal, as he began to talk fluently about her assets and bank accounts and so on.

Patsy sat quietly and felt within her a mounting tide of outrage and fury. How could he sit there like that, pretending that there had been nothing more between them than her finances? How dared he? Anger gripped her stomach, an anger she had never felt before. She said, loudly, into the middle of his speech, "You are a selfish, arrogant, and heartless man."

He looked up from his list of figures.

"I hate you," she said.

He put the paper down on the table. "What's the matter, Red?" he asked quietly.

He hadn't called her Red since he had entered the hospital. She stood up abruptly and went to stand before the empty fireplace, her back to him. "You're worse than Fred," she said in a voice she desperately tried to keep level. "At least he only stole my money."

Her emotions were in such a turmoil that she didn't hear him rise and cross the room toward her. Then his hand was on her shoulder and he was turning her to face him, and she could no longer hide the tears that were pouring down her face.

"Sweetheart," he said on a long note of wonder and surprise, and took her into his arms.

Patsy turned her face into his shoulder. "You at least could have had the decency to give me a proper good-bye," she sobbed into his green knit shirt.

He held her gently for a long moment, cradling her trembling body close to him. "I thought it was the best thing to do," he said after a while. His hand came up to lightly caress her hair. "I had put you in such terrible danger. And the case was over. It just seemed best."

She had stopped crying. "Is that all I ever meant to you? A way to finally get Jack Garfield?"

The hand on her hair stilled. "Of course not."

There was a note in his voice that had not been there before and it emboldened her to raise her head and look at him. There was a white line around his mouth and his eyes were shadowed. He had sounded angry.

"I love you," she said simply. "I think you should know that. I don't want to burden you or make you feel guilty, but I want you to know that. I love you and that's something that's never going to change."

There was the sound of rain drumming on the

porch roof, but other than that, the room was profoundly silent. He gazed intently at her tearstained face, and deep within his own eyes a little flame began to burn. "Do you know I have dreamed all my life of one day hearing you say those words?" His voice was strained and a muscle flickered in his cheek. "All my life," he repeated.

She stared into the flame that was glowing in his eyes, then, as the meaning of his words struck her, her lips parted. "Do you mean that?" she asked, her voice deep and hushed and shaken.

His mouth twisted. "Almighty God. That you could ask me such a question."

Thunder crashed in the distance, but neither Patsy nor Michael appeared to notice. They were too busy gazing, in astonished wonder and gradually dawning belief, into each other's eyes. Then she raised tremulous fingers and touched his face gently, searchingly, like a blind person seeking to imprint the contours of his bones on her mind.

"But why?" Her voice was barely a whisper, barely audible above the drumming sound of the rain. "If that's true, then why did you go away from me like you did?"

"Self-protection, really. I've wanted you all my life, and then, finally, I had you, and I had to live with the knowledge that it was only temporary. It was almost worse than not having you at all."

"No. Oh, no." She was slowly shaking her head. "How could you be so wrong?"

"I don't know." He smiled with his lips but his

eyes remained grave. "The pain in my leg was a picnic compared to what I've been feeling over you."

She reached for him at that, holding him tightly enough to strangle him, and saying, "Oh, Michael, oh, Michael," over and over and over again.

A flash of lightning illuminated the whole room and, instinctively, Patsy jumped.

"It's all right," he said next to her ear. "It is, quite incredibly, all right." And he laughed.

At his words Patsy loosened her grip on him and leaned back to gaze at his face. It was blazing with a look she had never seen before. Thunder crashed above them and she linked her hands loosely behind his neck and smiled at him. He looked so much younger, she thought. Just like that, he looked so much younger.

"I never thought I'd marry anyone younger than me," she said.

"Are you proposing to me, Miss Clark?" Even his voice sounded different.

"You bet I am, chum. Right now. What do you say?"

He grinned. "You do me a great honor—"

"Oh, shut up," she said rudely, "and kiss me."

He complied almost instantly. Five minutes later he raised his head and said huskily, "You pack a bigger wallop than this storm does, sweetheart."

"You inspire me," she murmured. Her eyes were heavy-lidded and very dark, her cheeks were flushed.

"Let's go to bed," he said, the hawklike look on his face extremely pronounced.

"Mmm," Patsy breathed, "I thought you'd never ask."

She had thought that nothing could be better than the passion they had shared previously, but she found, to her enchanted astonishment, that she was wrong. His touch was so gentle. How could such gentleness be so incredibly erotic? He looked at her as if she were a miracle and, for him, she felt like a miracle—a miracle of love, of passion, of surrender. "Oh, Michael," she whispered, "how I love you."

"Patsy." He entered her easily, his hands still caressing the smooth creaminess of her waist, her hips. He kissed her neck, her shoulders, her throat, and began to move inside her very slowly. It was like going mad with pleasure, building and waiting, building and waiting, a master musician orchestrating his symphony to the final crashing conclusion of wild, exultant, soul-shattering triumph.

After a long time Patsy, cradled close against him, heaved a great sigh. He laughed deep in his throat. "Feeling good?"

"Feeling fabulous. As well you know." She turned her head and kissed his bare shoulder. "You didn't hurt your leg?"

"I have no idea. If I did, it was worth it."

She sat up. "Let me look." The healing scar looked perfectly normal, so she lay back down again. "Looks okay," she reported. "It's a darn good thing that bullet didn't get you a few inches higher."

"I've thought of that possibility many times," he said fervently. "Believe me."

She chuckled and settled her head comfortably into the hollow of his shoulder. "Mother will be out of her mind with joy," she offered after a minute.

"Why?"

"She has been praying for me to get married for years. She never approved of my modeling, you know. 'So terribly public, Patsy dear.' "

Michael laughed at her imitation of her mother's accent. "Modernism was never your mother's strong suit."

"Emphatically not," Patsy said.

"I'll tell you something my mother once said to me, though," he offered. "She said, 'When you consider that Patsy is the only child of older parents and when you consider what a spoiled selfish brat she could have turned out to be, you have to take your hat off to Anne Clark.' "

"Well, my mother's most recent comments about you weren't nearly so complimentary. She was furious with you for getting me kidnapped. Couldn't understand it at all. 'Michael was always such a responsible boy,' she kept saying. But she'll be pleased as punch with you if you marry me."

"I'll promise her most faithfully never to get you kidnapped again."

"Thank you, darling. I would appreciate that."

He kissed the top of her head and she continued on a note of inquiry. "Did you mean what you said before—about loving me all your life?"

"I did."

"But you never once hinted . . ."

"There wouldn't have been any point. You never thought of me in that light. There was always that damn year between us in school." He was right. She never had thought of him in anyway that was remotely romantic. "Do you know when I first realized that I loved you?" he asked.

"When?"

"It was when we were still in junior high. You and Sally and I were walking home together from school one day and we saw an old man lying at the side of the road. There was a bunch of kids standing not far away, staring and making comments. The old guy was obviously drunk." He raised himself a little so he could see her face. "Do you remember what you did?"

"Of course. I thought he might be hurt and I went over to him to see if I could help."

"You did. And it turned out he had cut his head on the curb when he fell. And you sat down there right in the street, and put his dirty, smelly old head in your lap, and told me to call for help." He smiled at her. "It was then that I knew I loved you. And no matter how hard I tried, I've never been able to love another girl since."

She looked into his eyes. "But, Michael, if that's true, then why were you so standoffish when we met again?"

"Was I?"

"You know you were. That first night. I did have to seduce you."

He kissed the little crease of bewilderment that

furrowed her brow. "I was afraid," he said. "When you've wanted something for so long, all your life almost, and suddenly there it is—all you have to do is reach out your hand and take it—it's frightening."

"Oh, darling." Her voice was very soft. She reached up and touched the lean cheek that was so close to her. "Sally thought you loved Jane and that she jilted you."

He sighed and laid back on his pillow. "No. The person who got hurt in that relationship was Jane. She expected to marry me, and she had every reason in the world to expect it. But in the end, I couldn't. It wouldn't have been fair to her. I put in some pretty bad nights over Jane, I can tell you. She didn't deserve to get hurt. I was so glad to see her with her family the other day. Salved my conscience, you might say." There was a trace of bitterness in his laugh.

"I know." Patsy's voice was perfectly sober. "It's just wretched, having to hurt someone."

"You're quite a gal, Miss Clark." He picked up her hand. "No wonder half the world's in love with you."

"No," Patsy said, "they're in love with my face."

"I love that too," he said reassuringly, and Patsy laughed.

"Are you really safe from Garfield, Michael?" she asked after a bit, changing the subject.

"Yes. It's not as if my testimony was essential at his trial. The Justice Department has all the paperwork."

"I suppose you're going to continue with your dangerous career of catching thieves?"

"Well," he answered reasonably, "it's my job."

"Most accountants don't end up having guns pointed at them."

"It's not something I make a habit of myself."

Patsy sighed. "Oh, well, far be it from me to interfere with your job. Only I would appreciate it if you would exercise a little caution in the future. I have a stake in your well-being now, you know."

"A girl in a million," he said reverently, and kissed her hand.

"I suppose I'll have to move in with you. The way you complain about New York traffic, I don't see you commuting from my place."

"Well, no." He sounded amused.

"I don't like to sound snobby, Michael, but this house is ghastly."

"You can fix it up however you like."

"I have a better idea. If you can salvage some of my money, we can buy our own house on the beach." There was a small silence and she turned her head. "I hope you're not going to object to using my money?"

"The thought never occurred to me. I was just running some properties through my mind."

"You." It was her turn to lean up on an elbow so she could watch his face. "Enjoy it while you can, my friend, because the flow of modeling money is shortly going to stop."

He raised his brows. "Oh? Why?"

"Once I fulfill my present contracts, I'm retiring,

that's why. I'm going to do as Mother has alway
wanted, and stay home and cook dinner for m
husband."

He looked horrified. "Do you mean you're goin;
to make me support you?"

She grinned. "Yep. But for a dowry, I'll buy you
house."

"Well . . ." he said, considering.

"A big house. I want a lot of children."

"I'll have to raise my fees."

"And we'd better start soon. The sands of tim
are running out, you know. In two years I'll b
thirty . . . Michael!"

He had pushed her down on her back, and nov
his shoulders loomed over her.

"You just told me you wanted to start soon," h
said. "I'm only trying to oblige."

"You nut." She laughed at him. "Be careful o
your leg."

"The hell with my leg. It's another part of m
that concerns me at present."

Patsy's eyes widened as she felt what he was talk
ing about. "Oh, my. I see what you mean."

"Now," he murmured, his weight pressing he
back against her pillows. "You were saying some
thing about babies?"

Her arms reached up to encircle him. "So I was.
And she drew his head toward hers. "Darling, so
was."

YOUR CHOICE OF TWO
RAPTURE ROMANCE
BOOK CLUB PACKAGES.

.) Four Rapture Romances plus two Signet Regency Romances

or

) Four Rapture Romances, one Signet Regency Romance and one Scarlet Ribbons Romance

hichever package you choose save $.60 off the combined cover prices us get a free Rapture Romance, for a total savings of $2.55.

To start you off, we'll send you four books absolutely FREE e total value of all four books is $7.80, but they're yours *free* even you never buy another book.

So order Rapture Romances today. And prepare to meet a different ed of man.

YOUR FIRST 4 BOOKS ARE FREE!

Just Mail The Coupon Below

- -

Rapture Romance, P.O. Box 996, Greens Farms, CT 06436

ase send me the 4 Rapture Romances described in this ad FREE and without igation. Unless you hear from me after I receive them, send me 6 NEW Romances preview each month. I understand that you will bill me for only 5 of them h no shipping, handling or other charges. I always get one book FREE every nth. There is no minimum number of books I must buy, and I can cancel at any e. The first 4 FREE books are mine to keep even if I never buy another book.

h month please send me package ( )A   ( )B

───

lame   (please print)

───

ddress   City

───

tate   Zip   Signature (if under 18, parent or guardian must sign)

offer, limited to one per household and not valid to present subscribers, expires June 30, 1984. Prices ct to change. Specific titles subject to availability. Allow a minimum of 4 weeks for delivery.

RAPTURE ROMANCE

Provocative and sensual, passionate and tender— the magic and mystery of love in all its many guises

NEW TITLES AVAILABLE NOW

(045

#101 ☐ **ROMAN CANDLES by Ellie Winslow.** Ricardo Franco, Ital hottest rock star, wanted record executive Annie Rawli And though painful memories warned her to beware of man surrounded by glitter, it was too late. As the dazzli fireworks of his kisses lit up her life, Annie watched hers being swept into the blaze of a too-fantastic-to-be-true love . . (130162—$2.25

#102 ☐ **A FASHIONABLE AFFAIR by Joan Wolf.** When supermo Patsy Clark found herself involved with a crooked investme syndicate, she turned to childhood friend Michael Melville. former federal agent, he was just the man to protect her—a the lover who made her forget all past romances. But af this case was closed, would he still want Patsy—or would s just be his old pal "Red" again . . . ? (130170—$2.25

#103 ☐ **BEFORE IT'S TOO LATE by Nina Coombs.** Champi bullrider Garth Kincannon was the ideal subject for anthi pologist Liz Landry's study of rodeo cowboys. And though was infuriatingly chauvenistic, a night of wild passion show Garth could be a sensitive lover, too. But a cowboy's life v built around "going down the road." Could Garth change rambling ways—or was Liz riding for the hardest fall of life . . . ? (130189—$2.2

#104 ☐ **REACH FOR THE SKY by Kaser Adams.** At last! A roma from his point of view. Unpredictable Kitty Larkin promis just the kind of turbulence flight instructor Brenden Mor tried to avoid. But her fiery beauty was too powerful, a after a soaring night of passion, he wanted to bring th romance down to earth—even though he knew it'd be toughest landing he'd ever make . . . . (130197—$2.2

*Price is $2,75 in Canada.
To order, please use coupon on last page.

RAPTURE ROMANCE

*Provocative and sensual,
passionate and tender—
the magic and mystery of love
in all its many guises*

COMING NEXT MONTH

SILVER SEASON by Diane Carey. Rebecca Wyler had always felt fulfilled as a successful midwife, but that was before Dr. Drew Ironton had awakened in her a buried need for a different kind of commitment. It was ironic that Becca should fall for the conservative physician who was so opposed to her work. But as she became lost in the power of his magnetic sensuality, Becca wondered if loving would mean abandoning the career she believed in. . .

MISSISSIPPI MAGIC by Jillian Roth. The *Gateway* was a river barge, not a loveboat, and Katelyn Kennedy was its captain, not just a beautiful woman. Deckhand Christopher Carpenter would have to remember that— but it wasn't going to be easy for either of them. Katelyn sensed something unusual about him, and soon discovered he was the wealthy son of her fiercest competitor. But not soon enough to keep her from falling for her handsome rival. Christopher said he hadn't signed on to spy on her, but he'd said a lot of things that weren't true. . .

CATCH THE BRASS RING by Kasey Adams. Antique dealer Andrea Johannsen was searching for a long-lost nineteenth century carousel whose magnificent horses had been carved by her own grandfather. She never suspected that when she found it, she'd lose her heart to its handsome owner, Kirk Forrester. Would the price of mixing business with emotion put love as far out of Andrea's reach as the brass ring on her precious carousel. . . ?

MAGIC TO DO by Melinda McKenzie. *At last! A romance from his point of view!* What disturbed Paul Sand most at the Psychic Fair wasn't the phony fortunetellers. It was his chance encounter with beautiful Dr. Kirsten Anderson, when Paul felt the instant magnetism that draws two people together across time and space. Like Paul, she was a talented scientist. But unfortunately, her job was to expose him as a fraud! Instead of his soulmate, she could become his enemy, unless his love could change her doubting heart. . . .

RAPTURE ROMANCE

Provocative and sensual,
passionate and tender—
the magic and mystery of love
in all its many guises

Titles of Special Interest from
RAPTURE ROMANCE

RAPTURE ROMANCE

Provocative and sensual,
passionate and tender—
the magic and mystery of love
in all its many guises

97 ☐ LOVE AND LILACS by Kathryn Kent. (130111—$2.25)*

98 ☐ PASSION'S HUE by Anna McClure. (130138—$2.25)*

99 ☐ ARIEL'S SONG by Barbara Blacktree.
(130146—$2.25)*

#100 ☐ WOLFE'S PREY by JoAnn Robb. (130154—$2.25)*

*Price is $2.25 in Canada.

RAPTURE ROMANCE

*Provocative and sensual,
passionate and tender—
the magic and mystery of love
in all its many guises*

**Buy them at your local
bookstore or use coupon
on next page for ordering.**

RAPTURE ROMANCE

*Provocative and sensual,
passionate and tender—
the magic and mystery of love
in all its many guises*

(0451)

#65	☐	WISH ON A STAR by Katherine Ransom.
		(129083—$1.95)*
#66	☐	FLIGHT OF FANCY by Maggie Osborne. (128702—$1.95)*
#67	☐	ENCHANTED ENCORE by Rosalynn Carroll.
		(128710—$1.95)*
#68	☐	A PUBLIC AFFAIR by Eleanor Frost. (128729—$1.95)*
#69	☐	DELINQUENT DESIRE by Carla Neggars.
		(129075—$1.95)*
#70	☐	A SECURE ARRANGEMENT by JoAnn Robb.
		(129088—$1.95)*
#71	☐	ON WINGS OF DESIRE by Jillian Roth. (129091—$1.95)*
#72	☐	LADY IN FLIGHT by Diana Morgan. (129105—$1.95)*
#73	☐	AFFAIR OF THE HEART by Joan Wolf. (129113—$1.95)*
#74	☐	PURELY PHYSICAL by Kasey Adams. (129121—$1.95)*
#75	☐	LOVER'S RUN by Francine Shore. (129628—$1.95)*

*Price is $2.25 in Canada.

Buy them at your local bookstore or use this convenient coupon for ordering.

NEW AMERICAN LIBRARY
P.O. Box 999, Bergenfield, New Jersey 07621

Please send me the books I have checked above. I am enclosing $_____
(please add $1.00 to this order to cover postage and handling). Send check
or money order—no cash or C.O.D.'s. Prices and numbers are subject to change
without notice.

Name_____

Address_____

City _____ State _____ Zip Code _____
Allow 4-6 weeks for delivery.
This offer is subject to withdrawal without notice.

RAPTURE ROMANCE

Provocative and sensual,
passionate and tender—
the magic and mystery of love
in all its many guises

(0451)

RAPTURE ROMANCE

Provocative and sensual, passionate and tender— the magic and mystery of love in all its many guises